LAB RATS

Stuart Spitalnic

always for Debbie

LAB RATS

And ye shall know the truth, and the truth shall make you free.
John 8:32

8

PART 1

End of the Line

1

I don't yet know if I'll win or lose. I've had it all and then nothing so many times, I don't know which would be more right. My trial is almost over, and I could end up with less than nothing - ruined, bankrupt, alone. For anything I may have done, I can't deserve that.

It started with Millikan.

Hey, it's my story, and if I say it starts with a long-dead physicist, then that's how it starts. If you were following the case, some of what I'm about to tell you might repeat what you heard in court, but not most of it. The trial was just about the last part. Now that we're just waiting for the jury, I get to tell my story from the beginning - at least from what I call the beginning. I've had a long time to go over how it came to this. I keep getting back to Millikan.

It wasn't that long ago I read in a science journal (It might have been a *New York Times* story covering an article from a science journal, but either way.) that Millikan's oil-drop experiment is one of the top ten "most beautiful" experiments of all time. It's in pretty good company. Among the others were Galileo's falling bodies, Newton's work with prisms, and Cavendish's measurement of gravity. There were some big time names in the runners-up as well.

Millikan's oil-drop experiment came in at number three. The article said it had the beautiful simplicity of a classic scientific investigation. The experiment definitively demonstrated the profound notion that electrical charge is quantized, and in a way simple enough to repeat in a science class. The article called Millikan's experiment one of the most elegant experiments of early modern physics.

I hate the fucking thing.

In court they only wanted to hear about stolen drugs, falsified reports and buried data. The only thing that mattered to them was what happened, not why. I'm not saying I blame a dead physicist for what I did or for the trouble I'm in, but I do say my story starts with Millikan.

Millikan died long before I was born; he was 85. A lot of those turn-of-the-century, Nobel Prize winning physicists lived a long time. You would think after careers of shooting x-rays and gamma rays around without much by way of protection, they all would have died young. Some did; some developed the cancers you would predict they should have from their exposures, but most of those Nobel laureate physicists beat the odds. Maybe that gold medal with Alfred Nobel in profile has some protective power. Most of that generation of physicists lived a long time, and, thanks to their discoveries, they live on.

Robert Millikan measured the charge of an electron. He atomized oil into tiny droplets that would pick up an electrical charge. The droplets were introduced into a chamber with electrified plates. By adjusting the electric field between the plates, the oil droplets could be suspended or caused to float up or down. From the rate the droplets traveled at different voltages, Millikan could determine the charge on a given drop, and by determining the lowest-common denominator of charge, he could determine the charge on a single electron. His number turned out to be pretty close to the number used today, and he won the Nobel Prize.

The more I've looked the more I've found that it is the rare scientific advance that isn't associated with some kind of scandal. It would disappoint those who think of the Giants of Science as patch-jacketed, pipe smoking, disinterested intellectuals who pursued great truths with one percent inspiration and ninety-nine percent perspiration, but their rivalries and paranoias were fertile ground for enough scientific back-stabbing to make you wonder if they were pursuing the truth as much as they were pursuing the credit. Even Darwin rushed to publish his theory of evolution after he was asked to review a manuscript that would have scooped Darwin if it had been published first. Imagine if all the bumper stickers of a Jesus-fish sprouting legs said *Wallace* instead of *Darwin*.

Rosalind Franklin's x-ray photographs were essential to the discovery of the structure of DNA, and there has long been discussion over whether Watson and Crick relied on her results for their own findings, but she receives no general recognition for the discovery. Eventually, the structure of DNA would have been discovered, but who knows if, without Franklin, it would have been discovered when it had been, or if Watson and Crick would have been the ones to discover it. Franklin, who did not receive the Nobel Prize, died of cancer at age 37.

Millikan worked with a graduate student named Fletcher. An article published after Fletcher's death (Fletcher lived 97 years - another physicist who wouldn't die) suggests the whole oil-drop thing began as Fletcher's idea, and Millikan talked Fletcher into giving up any credit. It will forever be known as the Millikan oil drop experiment, not the Fletcher oil drop experiment. It's supposed to be the facts that matter, not who discovers them, but we know better.

Unlike those real scientists, my high school physics teacher must have died young. I'm surprised Marvin Bates lived through my senior year. If the health reports from those CNN talking heads are right about anything that leads to an early death, that chain-smoking fat bastard must have kicked sometime in the 16 or so years since I last saw him.

Bates could have assigned me any of the experiments: Avogadro's, Nernst's, Faraday's, or any of a dozen other classics suitable for repeating in a high school science class. Millikan was just the luck of the draw. Of course I blame Bates more than Millikan.

And Professor Underwood could have done better for me. He should have known Biotechna was doomed from the start, and he'd been around long enough that he should have warned me about Pharma. A little more support at the end from Underwood would have been appreciated, too, but I guess with his retirement only a few months away, he must have felt like Rick in Casablanca: *I stick my neck out for nobody.* Even if Underwood did let me dangle in the end, at least at the beginning he was trying to help. Bates never gave a shit.

I know. You're looking for the details of a big pharmaceutical scandal, and I'm telling you about a high school science teacher, a college professor, and some dead physicists. I told you, I've been thinking about how I got here. You'll hear what 're looking for, but I know how the story goes and I'm starting with a fat, chain–smoking, high school physics teacher and the failed duplication of a classic experiment.

Most of the world doesn't know about my trial. They didn't allow cameras in the courtroom, and the story, when it has been in the papers, hasn't been front-page material. There's been a gag order covering the details to prevent damage to Pharma's financial interests, so the whole story might never get out. I'm sure after today's closing statements, something will make the news, but it will be only a couple lines about the case and later, something about the verdict. This is my story.

I'll never forget the charge on an electron: 1.60×10^{-19} coulombs. That's a zero, a decimal point, then eighteen zeros before you get to a 16. I spent a semester in Bates's physics class trying to make up a number close enough to Millikan's to make it look like I had done some experimenting, but not so close that it would be obvious that I just made up the data. The other number in my head right now is a 17 followed by six zeros. That's 17 million. Pharma says my activities have cost them 17 million dollars and they just tried to get a jury to agree with them.

Kate's been on my mind too. She didn't come up during the trial, and she shouldn't have, but she's as much of my story as Bates, Underwood, and those damn lab rats. If I do get another chance with Kate, it wouldn't be because I deserve it.

I don't believe in predetermination. I don't believe everything happens for a reason. I don't believe in karma, good or bad. I don't believe that what goes around comes around, and I don't believe that everyone gets his due. I do believe we make our choices, and to that extent, we control our own destinies. On the other hand, it's funny how one thing always seems to lead to another.

PART 2

Longstreet High

2

Longstreet High was the only school in New York, and probably the only school in the northern United States, named after a Confederate army general. When they were building Longstreet, every new school on Long Island was being named after a long gone Indian tribe, but the superintendent wanted the new school's name to have a war hero motif. No one was ever quite sure why he picked Longstreet, but he pushed the name through the school board, giving impassioned speeches highlighting Lieutenant General James Longstreet's West Point education and noting that many authorities considered him responsible for the outcome at Gettysburg. After the final name was approved and released to the public, a group of Civil War buffs demanded the superintendent's resignation, noting that, among other things, General Longstreet was a Confederate general and, although he is often given some credit for the North's winning at Gettysburg, it is his incompetence that is blamed for the South's loss.

A few years after I graduated, the school's name was finally changed, and a few years after that, the district consolidated, and my old high school became a special education facility (special as in little-yellow-buses special) named for one of the discoverers of the structure of DNA. I don't remember if it was Watson or Crick (but I'm sure it wasn't that Franklin woman). The bottom line is, the high school I went to, the high school where I had Marvin Bates for sixth-period Advanced Physics, no longer exists.

There is no question that Marvin Bates – or Dr. Bates, as he insisted everyone call him – did not want to be a high school physics teacher. He wanted to be a cowboy. Not just any cowboy, he wanted to be a suburban version of the Marlboro Man. You remember the Marlboro

Man: tall western guy in a tan cowboy hat, matching leather vest. He wore a denim work shirt and jeans (always Levi's or Wrangler, never Sassoon or Jordache). The Marlboro Man was tan – not from sitting out in the sun, but from honest, hard work at the ranch. He wasn't a beautiful person in the current metrosexual definition of male attractiveness, but he had those rugged good looks that went right down to the bottom of the cracks in his leathery skin. The cracks weren't just wrinkles, but deep crevasses that came from working in the sun and taking long contemplative draws on the only smoke that would do: Marlboros. The Marlboro Man, at least the Marlboro Man before the Marlboro Man got lung cancer and died, is what Marvin Bates aspired to.

Dr. Bates was tall – you had to give him that – but he had to be as many inches around as he was high. He did have a tan leather cowboy hat and a matching vest, but the vest's two front panels could never reach each other around his girth, and much of the vest was invisible in the fold between his pendulous man-breasts and his enormous belly.

And, he sweat. By sixth period a lot of teachers might have little dark stains under their arms, or maybe on a hot day, their foreheads would shine a bit under the fluorescent lights. In the television commercials, back when cigarette ads were allowed on TV, even the Marlboro Man's head would glisten in the campfire as he and the boys enjoyed a pre-bed smoke. But when I tell you Bates sweat, I mean he *sweat*. You could tell time by his shirt. The sweat stain would be visibly creeping out from under his armpit by the time he made it from the parking lot to his first-period class, and quitting time for the day was always in sight when the sweat stains reached his shirt buttons.

If the visual of a sweaty 400-pound high-school physics teacher stuffed into a cowboy costume isn't enough, he also spoke with a lisp. And not a subtle speech impediment. I'm talking a Saturday-morning-cartoon Tweety Bird style "I tawt I taw a puddy tat" lisp. The sweat that had beaded up on his forehead would roll down his jowls and into his ragged red-brown mustache From there the sweat would be aerosolized into fine mist that would spray into the first few rows of students with every sibilant sound.

To the smell of a fat, sweaty physics teacher add the odor of stale cigarette smoke (Marlboro, of course). No one knew exactly how much he smoked, though the best estimate was about five packs a day. In the morning when he got to school, there was a butt burning in the hand he used to swipe his teacher's parking lot card at the gate. He would crush (and I mean crush) that smoke when he got out of his red pick-up and light another for the walk from his truck. If there was time, and there was always time, he'd smoke another by the dumpsters outside the auto shop.

Invariably one of the auto-shop crowd would ask, "Hey, got a light, Mister Bates?" Mister Bates pronounced "masturbates" by the auto-shop crowd.

"It's Dr. Bates, punk. And students aren't supposed to be smoking," Bates would say. With each year the burnouts changed, but Bates maintained the same level of apparent anger for this daily ritual. "Punk" was Bates's word for anyone who bothered him, and almost every student, at some time, would have some reason for Bates to call him a punk.

Bates would smoke between periods, chain-smoke through lunch, smoke on the way back to his truck in the afternoon, and light another after he stuffed himself back into the cab of his pick-up for the ride home. He also – and this is part of what made it so easy to cheat in his class – took long cigarette breaks during the period. He would smoke during tests, he would smoke during reading time, and he would smoke while we were working on lab experiments. He was never in class for more than 15 minutes at a time before announcing that he was stepping out. I'm sure his smoking didn't slow down after school, and who knew how many he got in on his way to work in the morning, his way home in the afternoon, and forget about the weekends. He smoked a lot.

Bates had no redeeming qualities. He was physically repulsive, a bad teacher, and a mean person. It's always hard to know with people like Bates which of their un-endearing features came first and which developed as a result of the others, but to us in high school, that didn't matter. Bates hated us, and we hated him.

I can't say that nothing positive came from my year with Bates. One good thing, probably the only good thing about that time, was that after years of watching her from a distance, I got to spend some time with Kate Mason.

3

I grew up next to the rich people on Long Island. I'm sure the rich people were pissed when they found out the undeveloped field next to their mini-mansions was going to be the site of affordable starter homes on quarter-acre lots. It wasn't my fault the school committee and town council split my neighborhood, sending my street to school with the rich kids. If we had lived just a few blocks over, I would have gone to Salk Elementary, Sabin Middle (Polio was just beat when these were built), and Matinecock High School. (Back to the Indian names, though I doubt the Indians pronounced it the way we did: "My tiny cock.") I would have been with kids whose families' financial situations were more similar to my family's. The result of the school committee's district line was that I ended up one of the poorest kids in one of the wealthiest schools on Long Island. We weren't broke, and in a lot of other Long Island schools my family's means would have been considered average. It's just that compared to the other kids in my school, there was no comparison. I had the worst clothes, no car, and no chance of keeping up with the other kids. No Billy Joel or Madonna tickets. No expensive clothes. No fancy sneakers. Seems stupid now, but at the time it was a big deal.

The disparities between my and the other kids' families became even more noticeable any time of year when gifts were involved. Their holiday takes were orders of magnitude more extravagant than anything my brother or I would see. We always got clothes for holidays and birthdays so we'd have something to wear until the next round of holidays and birthdays, and even then, if we were lucky, it was discount-store irregular Izod polo shirts - and we weren't often lucky. Many girls from rich families got a nose job and a sports car.

One would be a sweet-sixteen present, the other a graduation gift; which was given first depended on which was needed more. After winter break they would share stories of removing the red bow from a new Camaro or the white gauze from a new nose.

Kate Mason didn't need a new nose, and, unlike many of the others who didn't need new noses, she didn't get one. Her family, better off than mine but not as well to do as those whose houses were higher up in the hills, got her a car, but it was a more sensible, used Nissan, not a 'Vet or a bitchin' Camaro. Even though I didn't get to know her before the second half of senior year, unlike the nose-and-Camaro girls who would actively avoid guys like me who didn't have varsity letters or the right car, I thought we could have at least been friendly if there ever was the opportunity for us to be together, which finally there was in Bates' sixth period physics. The other girls in Kate's crowd wouldn't have given me the time of day – then or now.

Not to say that Kate had much interest in me right away once we finally had a class together- it was still Kate, and it was still me. I knew that she had been dating a basketball player at the end of junior year, and at some point in senior year she no longer was. I'm sure I wasn't on her A-list (or B-list) when she found herself between boyfriends. If you looked at her, and then you looked at me, you'd figure she was out of my league. So would have she. So would have I.

In the beginning of the year I had tried some lame lines a few times to talk to her. It would have been great if chicks dug nothing more than having guys ask them questions about physics homework. One time I offered her an umbrella in class for protection from Bates's spit spray. (Her friends overheard my offer and told her I was a moron. She thought it funny, but moronic.) I never would have spoken more than a few words at a time to Kate if Bates hadn't put us both at the same lab table. Any guy in my class would have killed to be paired with her; it was like winning a lottery.

Although Bates was a pig, he did have excellent taste in high-school girls. He assigned seats and lab stations in his class. The seating chart was the result of Bates's private beauty contest, with the winners in the front row. These front-row seats were well within spit-spray range when Bates talked, but why would Bates care? From the looks of him, you would figure he was either unaware of, or did not care about, his appearance, though it is hard to believe that even he wouldn't have consider himself anything short of repulsive. If he got his jollies by having the good-looking girls sit up front, what could anybody do about it?

Lab table assignments were made according to Bates's aesthetic as well. Those girls whose behinds filled out their designer jeans in the most pleasing manner were awarded rear-facing lab benches closest to Bates's desk so he'd have something to ogle when he wasn't out smoking.

Although Bates was disgusting, that didn't prevent jealousy among girls who weren't awarded positions of honor. Sarah Sheckman- she needed a nose job - was beaming when she was promoted to the front row after her new face was unveiled. Becky Parker, who was bumped from the front row by Sarah, promptly demanded her family provide her with a new nose. The procedure didn't go so well, leaving her nose a bit deformed. Bates told Becky to switch lab benches with me in the back, and that's how I ended up sharing the space with Kate. Becky's new lab-table partner, my old one, was Chet, a guy whose only known life talent was the ability to armpit-fart any song on request. Becky was having a bad year.

Kate kept her front-row seat and her rear-facing lab table the entire year. Maybe someone should have reported Bates to the school board, but you couldn't criticize his taste.

4

"This project will determine one third of your final grade," Bates said.

The spit mist twinkled in the fluorescent lights as it floated over Kate's head. Those in the first row became like Pavlov's dogs, bracing for the spray on words like "third" and "final," even when they weren't in the line of fire.

"In this beaker," Bates continued, "are slips of paper numbered one to twenty-five. Sarah will come around with the beaker, and you will pick a number. When you get your number, find the corresponding box, and bring it to your lab station."

Bates waved Sarah up with his Pillsbury Dough Boy fingers. He left the beaker where Sarah would have to reach for it, making no attempt to be subtle as he looked her over.

The classroom was the same as every other classroom in the science wing at Longstreet High. At the front was a multi-paneled chalkboard – the kind where you could slide around the front sections to reveal fresh slates so you wouldn't have to be erasing all the time. The writing on the board always looked moth-eaten from Bates's spit. Bates stood behind a combination desk and demonstration table. His stool was tucked in the middle, and on either side was a small sink and a connection for a gas burner. Between the board and the desk was an aisle plenty wide for a normal-sized person, but with Bates's girth, frottage was unavoidable when one of the girls in the class would be asked to work something out on the board. The rows of desks came next, then the lab tables. The sides of the room were lined with posters featuring pictures of famous scientists, and under each poster was one of the scientist's famous quotes. Pasteur saying,

"Chance favors the prepared mind." Feynman saying, "The first principle is that you must not fool yourself – and you are the easiest person to fool."

I drew number fifteen from Sarah's beaker and found my box under a black-and-white poster of Einstein. You've seen it, I'm sure. It's shot from above and shows his wild hair and a goofy smile. Under the poster was his quote: "Only two things are infinite, the universe and human stupidity, and I'm not sure about the former." Einstein's and Feynman's posters were different from the others. Of the dozen pictures, only those two showed the subjects smiling.

I took box fifteen to my table and set it down opposite Kate. On top of a tangled nest of electrical cords and plastic tubing was an oil-stained and torn sheet of mimeograph paper from the blue-ink era, though long past its smells-like-it-can-get-you-high stage.

```
Millikan's Oil Drop Experiment

Refer to page 127 of the lab experiment book for
the setup of the equipment and an outline of the
steps you must follow. The purpose of this project
is for you to replicate the experiment that
determined the charge of an electron. Keep your
lab notebook with the steps you follow and the
results you get along the way. You will not only
be judged on your final answer, but on your lab
technique and the quality of the notes you keep.
In this box you will find:
  1) Power source
  2) Viewing chamber
  3) Atomizer
  4) Oil …
```

"What'd you get?" I asked Kate over my box.
"Nernst."
"Nernst?"
"Nernst. How 'bout you?"

"Millikan," I said.

"Millikan?"

"Looks like Millikan."

How smooth was I with the ladies? After confirming the names of our assigned scientists, I stood there slack-jawed, straining for something charming to say. Nothing came.

Every piece of equipment that came out of my box had a piece-loose rattle that make me wonder when the last time any of it had worked. Something was crusted over on the viewfinder of the viewing chamber. There was a dark stain on the bottom of the cardboard box where most of the oil had spilled. A spider crawled out of the plastic tubing.

"You are responsible for your equipment and for keeping your lab space organized," Bates said, reentering the classroom after a smoke. "After your experiment is complete, I expect the equipment to be put away in as good condition as it was found so it can be used next year. For today, make sure everything on your list is accounted for. That should take you to the end of the period."

Kate was unpacking her box, laying out and checking over a reaction chamber, a zinc electrode, a copper electrode, a salt bridge, and some meters. My eyes darted from her face to her chest, to her lab equipment, to her hips, back to her face, and quickly to my lab set up when I saw she was about to lift her eyes. What is the sense that tells people they're being looked at, and what makes the looker think the pose they assume when busted doesn't give them away?

"What?" she said.

"Uh…nothing…I was looking at… your volt-meter."

Smooth.

I finished unpacking my box, and although everything was accounted for, it looked more like trash than science equipment.

"Would you look at this crap," I said to Kate.

"Why don't you say something to Bates?"

"How's your stuff?"

"I think it's okay. My experiment looks a lot simpler than yours."

"You want to trade?"

"No way," she smiled. "Say something to Bates."

"You think he cares."

"I know he doesn't," she said, "but maybe he has some spare parts or another box or something. I wouldn't plug it in – the whole thing might blow up. Say something."

I thought about it for a minute. Bates was a prick, but anyone could see the gear I had was inoperable – if Millikan had equipment like that, he never would have figured out anything.

Kate was right. I raised my hand, "Dr. Bates, is there any chance…"

Bates was out for a smoke.

5

"Man, Kate is hot," I said to Ralph.

"You gonna ask her out?"

"I think she has a boyfriend."

"Who?"

"I don't know."

"Then what makes you say?"

"She must."

"Who?"

"I said I don't know."

"Wuss."

"Fuck you."

Ralph Hartman had been my best friend since third grade. We hung out almost every day after school. Ralph's father was a vice-president at a financial firm in Manhattan and rarely got home before 9 PM. Ralph's mother started taking evening classes at the community college when Ralph hit high school. Ralph's older brother had been at college and out of the house three years by the time we were seniors at Longstreet. We spent a lot of time after school at Ralph's house.

His family lived in the rich neighborhood next to my development. Riding my bike to Ralph's house was like that part in the Wizard of Oz where everything goes from black-and-white to color. I'd leave my neighborhood, turn my bike onto Central Street, and hope the Thomas's rottweiler-mix was tied up, a fifty-fifty proposition, and that fucker would chase me half a mile if it was loose. The houses on Central Street had the stigmata of the less well-to-do: Christmas lights up year round, cars perpetually being worked on (often on blocks), Madonnas in half-bathtubs on the lawns, folding chairs in the driveways. Halfway up Central to Strawberry Farm Estates, everything changed. The lawns were large and manicured. The walkways lined with knee-high stone or brick walls. Light-lined and often gated driveways ran from the street to stone paths that led to columned entrances. Purebred dogs lay on porches next to marble lions - maybe the dogs would lift their heads and curl their upper lips, but they would never give chase. Each house had a tennis court or a swimming pool – many had both. Ridiculous topiary designs gave some of the homes a Seuss-like quality, but also let the world know the owners had enough money for ridiculous topiary designs. But the mailboxes were on the opposite side of the street. That part I never got: rich people, fancy neighborhood, but they had to cross a sometimes busy road to get the mail.

Ralph's house was in Strawberry Farms, but it wasn't as excessive as most. The Hartmans did have both a pool and a tennis court, but the front of their house was comparatively understated. There was a black iron fence separating the Hartman's house from its neighbors, and a gently curving driveway, marked on the left with a large boulder with the numbers "146" carved into it.

It was a warm April day, and I wasn't home from school for a minute before I told my mother I was heading up to Ralph's house.

"What about your homework?" she asked as she did most days.

"I'll do it after dinner. I don't have much."

"Don't you have tests coming up?"

The AP exams – advanced placement – were in a month. If I did well enough, I could get credit for some 101 courses. It didn't matter much to me at the time, but at a few hundred dollars a credit, I can see now how it would have mattered to my parents.

"I'll do fine," I said. "And they're not for a month anyway."

"How are you going to get into medical school with an attitude like that?"

My branch of the family tree was behind the others. The progression was pretty well defined. The immigrant ancestors came over from the old country and settled in New York City according to their ethnic groups – New York is really more a sorting chamber than a melting pot. Once things crossed over to this side of the Depression, parents worked hard so their kids could have a better life. For the first generation of bettering, that meant the kids didn't have to leave school to make money for the family. For the next generation, it meant working hard to get a home in Levittown or Wantagh or some Nassau County suburb that was close enough to the city to get to work, but gave the next generation of kids a yard to play in. The pressure on the next generation was to "make something of themselves," to go to college and get a career instead of a job. My mother had two sisters, and my father had a brother – one lawyer, one doctor and one engineer. My father hustled fabric in the garment district for not so much money, and my mother kept the books part time at a local pharmacy. My parents had missed the elevator the rest of their siblings caught, and they felt some pressure to make sure my brother and I caught the next one.

"I haven't started college yet, don't worry about medical school."

"Did you know that Abe Weinstein has already been accepted to medical school?"

"It was an early acceptance program. He's also locked into $25,000 a year for eight years just for tuition – I thought that would be out of the question."

"You don't think we'd find a way?"

"I'm going to Ralph's."

"Can you tell me when you think you'll be home?"

It wasn't until I went to college and made calls home that I realized my mother only talked in questions. Even her answers to my questions were in the form of questions. She probably could have kicked ass on Jeopardy, but it was a pretty annoying way to have a conversation.

I wonder what she'd say if I told her the details of how I ended up in the trouble I'm in now. *"Why did you have to get involved with those people? Didn't you know you'd get caught?*" She could have been a good psychoanalyst, always with a question for an answer.

Ralph didn't take any of the advanced placement courses. He wanted to be a lawyer and was going to go to college in D.C. His family thought he should relax his senior year and not worry about getting college credits now. His parents said he would work hard later.

"I'm glad my physics class doesn't have a project," Ralph said.

"Your teacher seems pretty cool, too. She probably doesn't spit either."

"Better than that chain-smoking fat bastard you got. Is that spitting stuff for real?"

"The first couple of rows get wet."

"You get to talk to Kate much?"

Ralph knew I had had a crush on Kate for years.

"Not as much as I'd like to. But we just started sharing a table together. She's really hot."

"I know," Ralph said. "I've seen her."

"She is."

"You should ask her out."

"I'm sure she has a boyfriend."

"If you want my advice…"

Ralph always had some advice to offer, whether he knew anything about the subject or not. I'm sure he made a fine lawyer. I should Google him and find out where he ended up - we lost touch by the end of college.

Ralph's entire sexual knowledge during high school came from watching his neighbor's daughter entertain men in her family's swimming pool. There was a gap in the hedgerow through which he would see topless sunbathing, in-pool intercourse, and whatever else she would do when her parents were away and she thought nobody was watching. Or did she?

In those days the place to go to not meet girls was the roller rink. Disco was a few years dead on the radio by then, but it still lived on at the roller rink.

"Toot-toot. Yeah. Beep-beep," Would be blaring from the Klipsch speakers suspended by chains from the ceiling.

Ralph and I would see if there were any girls we recognized from school at the rink and pace ourselves that we might create a chance run-in. It never worked. Occasionally, we'd get more than a couple of sentences of talk out of some girls, but invariably a slow song would come on – the ones where couples would skate holding hands. "Okay, we'll see you Monday," they'd say, then head *en masse* for the girls' bathroom.

"I think they liked us," Ralph would say, believing it only a little more than I would, which would be not at all.

"Why don't you wait here and see if they come back." Sometimes he waited. They never came back.

There wasn't anything terribly wrong with us; it's just that there wasn't anything terribly special about us either. We weren't the school's losers. Every school has them, so I know you know who I'm talking about. But we certainly didn't fit in with the cool people either. We weren't on the varsity teams. I didn't have a car, and Ralph's used Chevy Citation wasn't exactly the 'chick-magnet' we would have needed at the time. At some point in our lives these things would matter less, but at the time they seemed like the only things that mattered.

"So how's your project going anyway," Ralph asked, checking his neighbor's pool through the shrubs to make sure he wasn't missing anything.

"It's not. I'm making better progress with Kate than I am with this project, and that's not much. I can't get it to work. Bates keeps telling me to follow the directions: 'Last year's class was able to do the project with the same equipment; you should be able to, too.' There ain't that much time left."

"Bates is an asshole," Ralph said.

"Last week Bates told me, 'It's the poor carpenter that blames his tools,' completely soaking me with spit then just waddling off to get a smoke in before the end of the period."

"What are you going to do?" Ralph asked, checking his neighbor's pool again for activity.

"I don't know. The project's due in two weeks. If I can't get it running I'm going to have to start making up some numbers."

"Cheating is wrong, *Daaaaavie*," Ralph said, in his best Davey and Goliath voice.

Davey and Goliath was this Sunday morning religious claymation show, in which Davey was always tempted to do something sinful, and Goliath, his dog, would always tell him what Father Brown would say when he found out. The lessons turned out to be a lot funnier when we watched the show while getting high in college. There was even a drinking game requiring a chug every time the dog said, *"But Daaaaavie..."* The show was on six-o'clock Sunday mornings, and we would still be up from the night before.

"Yeah, well what would you do?" I asked Ralph. "I'm like the only one who doesn't cheat on the tests. Bates doesn't spend ten minutes in the room during exams, and it gets as loud as Mardi Gras. I'm barely keeping up with the curve as it is. This project is one-third the grade. If I fail the project, I won't get the AP credit. If I can't get the project working in the next couple of days, I'm going to have to start making up the numbers. What would you do?"

"You want to know what I would do?"

"Yeah, what would you do?"

"You really want to know what I would do? Like you're asking me for advice?"

"Yes. What would you do?"

"If I were you..."

Ralph pressed his face deeper into the shrubbery to get a better view. There was a splash and some laughter from the pool next door; the show was about to begin.

"What, Ralph? What would you do?"

"If I were you... I'd ask out Kate."

"Asshole."

"That's what I'd do."

A girlish shriek of fake protest came from the pool next door, followed by a man's deep laughter. Ralph disappeared into the hedge.

"Thanks for the advice," I said. "Now move over."

6

The world didn't seem so sue-happy when I was in high school. Today, it seems the first step before doing anything is to figure out how to avoid getting sued. There was a time when you didn't have to sign a four-page medical waiver to rent a canoe. The risk of electric shock from using a toaster in a bathtub was considered well known. Coffee was understood to be a potentially hot beverage, warning label or not. Have we as a society become more safety conscious or more retarded?

When I was in high school the school board hadn't yet gotten the message that no student could be exposed to any possibility of harm. Do they still climb the thirty-foot rope in gym class? Do they let students operate the band saw in wood shop? Are students allowed to take the baked goods out of the oven in home economics? I don't know what the science classes are like today (simulated sharp instruments to dissect artificial frogs?), but it was a miracle nobody was killed in Bates's class.

Bates's physics lab was a free for all; the lawsuits that could have been generated just from my year could have bankrupted the district many times over. One time a gas forming reaction caused a glass stopper to shoot from a beaker, and it ricocheted around the room like a champagne cork in a winning team's locker room. The thing bounced off two walls and shattered on Kate's side of our lab table. One kid got a chemical burn from spilt hydrofluoric acid and spent the night in the hospital getting intravenous calcium infusions to keep his heart from stopping. A puddle of acetone fogged across one lab table and ignited on an Bunsen burner's open flame. The flash flame cost Lisa an eyebrow and necessitated her wearing eye patches for a week while her corneas healed.

Bates was out smoking for each of these events and during several near misses. He'd come back smelling smokier, his sweat stain a little larger. Unless someone was bleeding or really needed some medical attention, we covered for each other. Bates would ridicule the victim of an unfortunate lab accident; either he hoped the shame might keep people from fucking up, or he just didn't care. We couldn't cover for the eyebrow-fire incident.

"How many times do I have to tell you to be careful?" Bates yelled, spit flying from his face.

Bates returned from his smoke break to see Lisa clutching her face. The smell of singed hair was strong enough to overpower even Bates's perma-odor.

"My face! My face!"

"Why can't you kids be more careful?" Bates repeated. The blinded Lisa walked into her lab table and spun off the people next to her.

Bates walked behind his desk, crossed his arms, and sat on his stool, the stool's protesting creak audible over Lisa's crying.

"Becky, take Lisa to the nurse."

"Okay punks," he said after they left for the nurse. I hope you learned a lesson – you're supposed to be getting ready for the real world, and I got news for you, the real world is a dangerous place. Do I have to tell you again? Be careful. There's still some time left. Back to work."

We could hear the approaching ambulance as Bates left for a smoke.

If you look hard you can see two dark spots on my left thumb and index finger where I took some current from my experiment's faulty power cord. It was nothing like having your eyebrows burned off-Lisa's didn't grow back in time for graduation – but when I received that jolt, it removed all doubt as to whether or not I would be able to get my project to work. The equipment just wouldn't assemble. The pieces that did fit together wouldn't stay together. The oil was supposed to come out like the spray from a perfume bottle. Instead, it beaded up at the end of the tubing and oozed to the floor of the viewing chamber like snot. The hum that emitted when I plugged the thing in sounded just wrong. Everyone else was wrapping up their experiments. My notebook was empty. There was just no way.

The siren faded as Lisa's ambulance pulled away. Bates was long gone, smoking. I stood there staring at my failed equipment.

"Can you believe Bates?" Kate asked.

I froze. Since we started sharing a lab table, Kate was always polite, and we had had a few conversations, but I always initiated them with some lame one-line question I had thought up and practiced the night before. I think that was the first time she spoke to me without my first saying something. Maybe it was the stress of what just happened to Lisa's face– the burnt human-flesh smell still loomed – but I didn't care. I was transfixed. I stood there like a moron smiling my braces-just-off, two-toned-teeth smile like she had just brought me flowers.

"Yeah," I said.

"Walter?"

"Yeah?"

"I asked if you could believe Bates?"

"Yeah," I snapped out of it. "I mean no. Bates. What an asshole. He didn't even try to help her."

"Did you see her? It looked like part of her face was dripping off."

"I think she lost an eyebrow. I'm sure it will grow back. I didn't see any blisters or anything."

"There's only a few minutes left in the period," Kate said. "I'm done for today."

"It's too bad Bates wasn't here right when it happened," I said. "He could have spit the fire out."

She laughed.

She laughed! I had said something, and she laughed. I spent hours trying to come up with things to say that might make her laugh, always coming up empty. I was so impressed by my success I didn't realize I was staring at her. Staring through her really – lost in her dark hair, brown eyes, her perfectly shaped mouth that always made her look satisfied. Just beautiful and perfect and right there across the lab table. I could still be standing there now just staring at her if she hadn't said…

"What?" I was busted again for staring.

"Um…Nothing."

It became one of those now or never moments. I thought about it for a few seconds, but if I had thought about it for a few more, my guts and the opportunity would have slipped away. I went for it.

"Hey. You wouldn't want to…" I froze again.

"What?"

"Nothing."

"Oh."

"I mean…"

"What?"

"You wouldn't want to…forget it."

"Okay."

"What I mean is…"

"Walter, spit it out."

"You want to do something after school? Get something or something. Go somewhere?"

"I can't"

"That's Okay."

"Walter – are you asking me out?"

I hated her for saying that. She could have told me no and left it at that. She didn't have to torture me – I was surprised I came up with the balls to ask her, even as whimpily as I did. I didn't even know if she had a boyfriend or not. Was she trying to get me to dig my hole deeper so she could make fun of me later with her friends?

"It was just so crazy today," I said. "I can't get my thing to work, Lisa just burned her eyebrows off and I thought maybe you would want to…"

"Walter, I can't *today*. But maybe tomorrow."

"Maybe tomorrow?"

"Are you asking me out?"

"No, I mean, it's just...that things were so crazy today and...yes. Yes. That's what I'm doing. I'm asking you out."

"Then ask me."

"Kate, would you like to go out with me after school tomorrow?"

"Sure."

"Thank you."

"Thank you?"

"Thank you. You could have put me through all that and still said no."

"I wouldn't have done that," she said. "But it's nice to know I could have."

"I'm just surprised..." I stopped before I made it sound even more stupid.

"You wanted me to say no?"

"No."

"Tomorrow after school then."

"Yes."

"Where are you taking me?"

"Uh..."

"Will you be picking me up?"

Now she *was* torturing me. She knew I didn't have a car. I only had my learner's permit, and my road test wasn't for a couple weeks.

"I could have my mom take us." That sounded cool.

"How about I drive?" she said.

"That would be good."

"Good."

I carried a retarded smile with me the rest of the day.

"You did?"

"Yup."

"You are?"

"Yup."

I threw the Frisbee wide and it landed near the gap in the hedge, and Ralph did a quick check for topless sunbathing before getting it. Nothing yet.

"What are you going to do?" Ralph asked.

"I don't know yet. She's driving."

"Really?"

"Really."

"Is this going to be the start of something big?"

"I don't think so. We're just going out after school. We've been sharing a lab bench, and we're just going out after school. She probably has a boyfriend."

"Why is she going out on a date with you if she has a boyfriend?"

"It's not a date. Maybe her boyfriend is in college."

"Maybe there is no boyfriend." Ralph pumped his eyebrows up and down.

"Maybe."

"So, you gonna try and slip it to her?"

"Ralph!"

"I'm just asking. You've read those letters in my father's Penthouse, too. 'I always thought these letters were made up and that nothing like this could ever happen to me, and then one day…"

"Enough Ralph."

"Walter's in *luh-huv.*"

"We're just going out after school. It's nothing."

"You guys going steady now? Does this mean we can't hang out anymore? I've seen that happen. Guy meets a chick, next thing you know, he dumps his friends."

"Ralph, cut the crap and throw the Frisbee. I still bet she has a boyfriend."

"Then why is she going out with you?"

"I told you, we've been working together…"

"I know, I know. What about the prom?"

"What about it?"

"You going to ask her?"

"I doubt it. I'm sure she's already got a date."

"But you don't know if she has a date, do you?" Even then, when he wasn't talking sex, he talked like a lawyer.

"No."

"Walter's got a *girlfriend*."

"In a couple months we'll be hundreds of miles apart. She's going to Maine and I'm going to be in middle-of-fucking-nowhere New York, and that will be that."

"Whatever. How's that project going anyway?"

"It's not. It's due in two weeks, and I can't get the thing to work. I'm going to have to activate Plan 'B.'"

"I figured."

"You think it's wrong?"

"Of course it's wrong. But it doesn't look like you have much choice. Who's going to care anyway? You think twenty years from now it's going to make any difference if you cheated on a science project in high school? I think not."

I hasn't quite been twenty years, but yes, I do think it made a difference. I lost touch with Ralph when I was in grad school, but after this trial is over, I'm going to find him and remind him of what he said.

After Ralph made that remark, he checked the gap in the hedges again. Still nothing.

7

I was too distracted to pay attention in class. When I was at the lab table with Kate sixth period, I just moved the Millikan apparatus around – not that I could have gotten it to do anything anyway- but I could have given it another try. Kate was mixing solutions in her reaction chamber and weighing electrodes. I could have watched her do that for the whole hour. In fact, that's all I did do for the whole hour. She was going to Maine to major in English. She wanted to be a writer or get into publishing, but she worked that physics project with so much intensity, you would have thought science was her life and she was on the brink of some big discovery. At the time I thought it curious that she could be so serious about something she needn't consider important. Now, that draws me to her even more.

I did ask Bates for help one last time. I again assembled the apparatus, and it had the sturdiness of a house of cards.

"Marlon Frist had no problem getting it to work last year," Bates spit. "I've always suspected the students get a little dumber each year. Has it gotten to the point where you're too far over on the Darwin chart to follow simple directions?"

It was what I expected. I really didn't want to have to cheat- I know I was driven more by the avoidance of guilt than the desire to be moral, but, until then, I hadn't been a *cheater*. If I overheard an answer during a test, I would use the information, but I never sought that kind of help or peeked at someone's paper. But the only way I would get any results on this project would be to make them up.

I went through the motions so Bates would be less suspicious when I did turn in my paper- I don't suspect he cared or paid enough attention to be able to identify anything I might have given him as bullshit, but I couldn't count on his not getting enough pleasure from getting someone in trouble that he might try to nail a cheater. I squeezed the atomizer, forcing contaminated ooze from the tubing. I plugged in the electric plates. Sparks popped from the power cord. Bates was out for a smoke as the ozone smell filled the room. The eyepiece on the viewing chamber wouldn't focus, but there wasn't anything to focus on anyway. Three projects were already completed – the boxes packed away, the students excused from class and in the library writing up their results. It would be Kate's last day of work as well. The projects were due the end of the following week.

"So we'll go for ice cream," she said after she finished her last measurement. "Celebrate the end of the project."

"I don't think I'll be done today."

"Then we'll celebrate my finishing the project. Unless you want to skip?"

"No way."

In a sense, I was finished. The only thing left to do was pick a number close to the 1.6 X 10 E –19, get all the formulas together, and work backwards to fabricate the results I should have obtained by performing the experiments. What if it was a hoax all the way back? What if Millikan made up his shit, too? Show me an electron and tell me how you measure its charge.

I had to get the advanced placement credit, though. My parents were fighting about money every night as it was. Midstate was an expensive school, so it mattered if I got the credits. If I didn't cheat, I was looking at an "F" for the project. I had nothing to show for a few month's work. I didn't know who Marlon Frist was, but there was no way he got it to work the year before. He must have made up the results the way I was about to. I could hear Bates next year telling some sucker, "Well, Walter Most had some trouble, but he got it done on time. Your class is even dumber than last year's, and I didn't think that was possible..."

When I was writing up my made-up results, I remember wondering what the big deal was anyway. Bates was an asshole. I was only in the situation I was in because I picked Project Number 15. That wasn't fair. I *could* have done any of the other projects if I had picked them. It's not my fault I drew the clunker.

Once I committed to it, the cheating was easier than I thought it would be. For all my weighing whether or not I should hand in a fictional research project to avoid failing, I was able to finish my first draft over the following weekend. I decided my answer should be off by sixteen percent. I picked sixteen percent on my own. A couple of years ago- when I was briefly wealthy- an accountant friend of mine told me that when making up numbers for a tax return, never pick numbers that end in five or zero; they look made up even when they are not. He suggested changing the fives and zeros, even when they were arrived at honestly, to avoid raising suspicion.

My physics project had become a math project. I plugged my pre-selected solution into the formulas and worked backwards to generate the data that I should have gotten from the experiment. I spent the next Monday and Tuesday at my lab desk fiddling with the equipment- I still had to put some time in so Bates could believe my experiment generated something besides ozone.

"Mister Most," he said. "I see you finally got it going."

"Yes, Dr. Bates."

"See, I told you if you put some effort into it instead of complaining, you would get something done. Science is ninety-nine percent perspiration."

"Thank you," I said, trying not to laugh at the fat guy in the cowboy suit with huge sweat stains telling me the importance of perspiration. After his pep talk, he waddled out for a smoke.

The thing wasn't even plugged in. At least Bates caught me doing what at least looked like work. I would continue the charade for two more days, setting up the non-functional equipment and doodling in my lab notebook whenever Bates came in from one of his many smoke breaks. On the Thursday, I packed up my box of gear and away it went until next year, when some new sucker would draw number fifteen.

After school I met Kate outside her social studies class, and we walked to her car, a two-year old Nissan Maxima her parents gave her when she got her license. She drove us to the ice cream shop at the mall.

"You were quiet in Bates's class today," she said.

"There's not much time left. I had to get the rest of the data by the end of the week."

"You got it working then?"

I felt a shiver come over me. People cheated in school all the time, she knew that. Would she think less of me for cheating on the same project she had worked so hard on? I should have put more thought into whether I would start lying to her before we even had a first date. There are a million kinds of dishonest people, but there is only one way to be honest. She must have known I couldn't have possibly been doing any real work in class. She had to know. There was no good reason not to just tell her what I was doing. She wouldn't rat me out.

"What's that?" I said. Nice stall.

"The project. You get the results you need?"

"Yes, I got my results."

Was it a lie? I don't even know anymore. I do know that at the time, it felt worse telling Kate than it did cheating on the project in the first place. Was that how it worked?

We ate our sundaes. I didn't say much. I was going around and around in my head whether or not I should just tell her the truth – it seemed so stupid. At one point I felt my lips moving as I was talking to myself. She must have thought me a psycho.

"Walter, what's wrong?"

I froze. I didn't know what to say, so I said, "Do you want to go to the prom?"

"Yes. Did you mean with you?"

"Uh, Yes. I mean do you want to go to the prom with me?"

"I guess so." She smiled.

"You do?"

"Yes, I do."

It was a good cover for my silence. She would believe I was mulling it over in my head before asking her. In truth, if my thoughts weren't otherwise preoccupied, I never would have had the courage. And that made me feel even worse for the lying. I should have just told her everything right then. She would have been okay with it - it was just a stupid science project.

The longer it hung out there, though, the less likely it was that I would ever spill the truth. I know now that in the long run it's better to always tell the truth. Of course, who gives a crap what the guy getting his ass sued for fraud thinks about honesty? The hard part about always telling the truth is the *always*.

8

So I'm heading into class the morning that the physics project is due. I see Bates coming from the teacher's parking lot, cigarette in hand, and I know my walk and his waddle will get us to the door at the same time. Bates is the last guy you want to be paired with in one of those two-guys-stuck-in-a-door slapstick routines. He turned just before the main entrance and headed towards the dumpsters outside auto shop.

"Hey, Mister Bates!" Burnout #1 says, leaning on the dumpster. *Mister Bates* pronounced *masturbates*, as always.

"Look guys," Burnout #2 says, "It's Master Bates."

"Hey, Master Bates, you losing weight? You look good."

"It's Doctor Bates, punks, how many times do I have to tell you, it's Doctor Bates."

"Hey man, watch the spit, you gonna put our smokes out. Guys, Mister Bates says he don't masturbate."

Burnout laughter follows, and that's the last I can hear as I enter the building with my fabricated report tucked under my arm. If it was any other teacher, I would have felt bad for him. Bates had tried to get the dumpster crowd in trouble before, but it had no impact. They only stayed in school so their parents would let them live at home - if they went out on their own, they'd have to pay rent, and that would cut into their drug money. Some of them hung out at a house near Ralph's. A lot of the rich kids where I grew up turned into either condescending pricks, burnouts, or both. The rich kids could afford the most drugs. I guess the rich kids could afford to be condescending pricks, too.

I had written my report on our family's TRS-80. At the time, word processors didn't make word processing much easier than using a typewriter with a correction ribbon. Files were saved with tape recorders on cassette tapes that would invariably get recorded over. I lost a history paper once when my mother recorded a Men at Work tune off the radio.

>NO FILE FOUND

>Abort, Delete, Retry??????

I pulled the computer cable from the cassette player to hear Colin Hay singing about a Vegemite sandwich.

I was up pretty late writing the Millikan report. I talked to Kate on the phone for an hour and had to redo much of what I had thought was coming out well. She finished hers the day before and was putting some finishing touches on her cover page. I suggested she not burn the edges for that antiqued effect, like half the English class did for a Shakespeare paper. She wasn't going to.

My last chance to do the right thing was right before I turned it in. I could have confessed to Bates that the equipment didn't work, that there was no way it had worked for years. I was sure that close to a decade of students must have made up the data as I had – and I'm sure all of *them* did just fine in life. My parents would understand – they'd be pissed at first, but eventually they would be proud of me for doing the right thing.

I asked Ralph if he thought I should go to the principal and tell the whole story.

"Who knows, maybe Bates would be fired," I fantasized.

"Fat chance," Ralph said, spitting and holding his hands out to simulate Bates's girth.

I had typed up what, if the data had been honestly obtained, would have been a legitimate effort at a real scientific report. Hell, I got an B+ on it.

When it was due, I turned it in.

And nothing happened.

You would think, after telling you that this stupid physics project forms the foundation for the trouble I'm in today, that when I passed it in I would have felt something: the pressure of guilt, an excited rush, anything. I felt nothing. I put my paper on the pile on Bates's desk and took my seat. There was no sense of impending doom, no wish to run back and rip the paper and confess my sin. After I turned it in, my life did not become *Crime and Punishment*. I didn't feel people looking at me. I didn't imagine Bates around every corner, waiting to expose my deception.

I can't say I felt good about it, either. But that's just it: I felt nothing. Maybe that's what made it easy.

Kate and I went to a movie that weekend. The prom was in a couple weeks. Graduation would follow. Then summer, then college. There were two and a half months until college. After I handed in the report, all I cared about was figuring out how I could spend as much time as possible with Kate.

9

Kate and I didn't sleep together, not during that summer at least, but that wouldn't keep me from telling my new college friends that we had when they gawked at the picture of her on my desk. It was of Kate in a two-piece taken one day at Jones Beach – I still have it – it's *Sports Illustrated* worthy, and people had a hard time accepting that someone who looked like her would let me get close enough to even take a picture.

The prom was fun, but overrated. I have the picture of Kate and me at the prom somewhere, too, but that one doesn't compare to the swimsuit one I keep on display. At the time I remember thinking how good we both looked, but the eighties prom-wear was heavy on the *poof*, and my ruffle shirt and wide-lapel tuxedo seem more ridiculous each time I come across the photo.

Graduation, at least the ceremony itself, was painful. A couple hundred of us sat in folding chairs on the football field, listening to some local politician tell us how we were the future and the future was now. The parents filled the bleachers, all leaning over each other trying to get a clear shot of the back of our heads with microwave-oven-sized video cameras. Some were off to the side, calling distant relatives on toaster-sized cell phones. Compared to electronics now, that stuff looked like it could have came out of *The Flintstones* – can't you see Fred talking on one of those huge "portable" phones while the waitress puts the car-tipping portion of ribs on his window?

After graduation, my parents wanted me to go home with them, but I went with Kate's family.

"Don't you know your grandmother is coming in from Brooklyn, Walter?" my mother said. "Won't you come home?"

My grandmother coming in from Brooklyn meant that in the corner of the kitchen, in a wheelchair, would be a prune of a woman who could barely speak. If you could believe the black-and-whites, she was something to look at about the time of World War II. But as people who still tell stories from the Depression never seem to appreciate, the Depression was a long time ago. Now she wore diapers, babbled, and needed to be fed. You leave the world as you enter.

"She won't care if I'm there now or later," I said. "I'll be home later."

Except for the week Kate and her family went to Lake Winnipesaukee, we saw each other every day. Ralph went to some summer prep program in Vermont, so I didn't have to feel bad about blowing him off. I would have blown him off to be with Kate, if I had to make the choice, but I didn't have to.

Kate would pick me up in the morning, and we'd head to the beach. I passed my road test, but my family could never afford an extra car, and certainly not insurance for another car with a seventeen-year-old male driver on Long Island. Sometimes I drove my mom's car, but the coolness of driving only briefly made up for driving my mom's wagon, so I was fine with Kate driving. For spending-money I had a job at the mall two nights a week. Otherwise, I would be at Kate's house most evenings, too. Kate's parents told her this was her last summer of "freedom" and that she didn't have to work if she didn't want to. I was getting a hard time for not working more.

We never talked about our going away for college until the very end. We knew we would have to, but we never let it come up. There would be more than four hundred miles between our schools, most of it highway, but still, too much driving. The first real conversation we had about the distance was three days before we both would leave. We got dinner at a Friendly's after an evening's shopping for college stuff.

"It's only like a seven-hour drive you know," she said, knowing I'd know what she meant.

"I know."

"It would only be like a one hour flight," she tried to smile.

"Are there even airports near either of our schools?"

Midstate was an hour west of the New York Thruway in the middle of Upstate New York. Kate's school was similarly positioned in Maine. I did check– there was no air-service connecting the two cities that would take much less time than driving.

"I don't think I can afford to fly, anyway," I said. "I could take a bus, though. I'm starting with nine AP credits, so I'm only taking twelve first semester." That reminded me of the "B+" I got in Bates's class and on the Millikan project. I passed the advanced placement exams.

"Maybe we can meet in the middle, sometimes" she said.

"Have you looked at a map? I don't think there is a middle."

"We'll figure something out,"

So, we're sitting there in Friendly's, she has a straw in her mouth, her head is turned down over a Coke, and she's looking at me over her soda. Her hair falls from behind one of her ears and swings in front of her face, partially covering one of her eyes. She laughs, then I laugh. When I think about her now, and now I think about her a lot, that's how she's looking at me.

PART 3

Midstate University

10

I watched New York's drinking age go from 18 to 21, and never would be legal until my senior year of college. When I came of age, there was some satisfaction in being able to buy beer legally, although no bar or liquor store in Midstate's college town checked IDs anyway. Even when they did, at the time an X-acto knife, a photocopier and some blue eye shadow could make a convincing of-age New York State drivers license. Now everything is digital, and bars scan holographic licenses into computer databases to identify counterfeits.

I was fifteen the first time I got drunk. Ralph's parents didn't drink, but every December his family's liquor cabinet would be restocked with bottles of cheer that made their way around his father's office. Anything that had been opened was fair game. Tap water kept the fill-levels steady after our withdrawals, and anything in the fridge served as an emergency mixer to cover the taste of the less palatable liquors. We learned some chemistry too: milk and citrus don't mix (the milk curdles), and nothing covers the taste of bad (or good) tequila.

It's different at college now. Even the fraternities are mostly dry. I went back to my old fraternity house for an alumni weekend a couple years back and asked for a gin and tonic. They looked at me like I asked where the kiddie porn was kept. 'Shrooms, GHB and ecstasy were everywhere, but they would sooner keep plutonium in the house than Southern Comfort. There were posters all over campus warning of the stiff penalties for being caught with alcohol.

When I was an undergrad, the only recognized danger of drinking was standing too close to someone who was about to hurl. Drink too much, pass out on a couch, and you might find yourself mummified in toilet paper or missing an eyebrow, but in general, the sport was considered harmless.

Before college, the only concept of fraternity life I had was from sneaking into *Animal House* with Ralph. We wouldn't reliably be let into the R rated movies, so we bought tickets to something else that started at the same time and entered the theater on the right instead of the left. A victimless crime.

My first exposure to Midstate Greek life came the night before classes started. I was dutifully looking at my class schedule and the campus map, trying to figure out when and if I would need to set my alarm clock, when I first heard them. It started as a dull vibration, then a pause, then more vibration. The vibrations got louder and louder, then the pauses were filled with voices, then the pounding shook the walls between the next room and mine, then it was my door.

I opened the door, and fifteen guys in *Theta Theta Tau* sweatshirts spilled into my room. They were having a rush party after the first day of classes and promised plenty of beer and women. A drunk one with a mustache picked up the picture of Kate off my desk- the one of her in that bikini.

"Whose the chick? She's hot."

"That's my girlfriend from home."

"Where is she now?"

"Maine."

"She's really hot. Shouldn't have left her behind. No chance. Sorry."

"Hey, give him a break." There was a hint of a beer-induced slur from the tallest of the bunch, who turned out to be the chapter president. "He just got here. He'll learn."

He handed me a blue sheet. On one side was a photocopied map to the house, on the other was a cartoon of a drunk-seeming Calvin from Calvin & Hobbes raising a beer mug.

"Thanks," I said, taking the map.

"We'll see you tomorrow."

They filed out and continued the process next door. The mustached one paused before leaving.

"You like to get high?"

I froze. I didn't know the right answer. It sounded like something I should answer "yes" to. Until then, the real answer was no. I would, but I hadn't.

"Uh, sure," I said.

He smiled. "Show up tomorrow."

I started college pre-med. I was fulfilling the evolution from immigrant to professional that started with my great-great grandparents. I was often reminded growing up how they were professionals in the old country before giving up everything so I - not to be born for another seventy years – could have a chance at a better life. Everyone's family offered them the same story; they were doctors, lawyers, and politicians. But they came to America and had to iron clothes and deliver meats. Generations of hard work and sacrifice so I could be where I was: a pre-med freshman biology major at Midstate University.

The Biology Department lecture hall had two hundred seats arranged in concentric semicircles of floor-bolted swivel chairs behind concentric semicircles of Formica-topped desks- the design worked unless there was a full house and more than five lefties. Each seat pointed towards the center of the circle, where there was a speaker's podium. Behind the speaker were chalkboards set up like the ones in Bates's class, but with more panels. Notes could be put up on the back-most boards and be shielded until they were needed. There were fourteen panels in a four-tier system and, invariably, a complicated concept would be made even more complicated by the professor forgetting the order in which the boards were supposed to be revealed. We wouldn't see that happen for a while. On the first day of class the only thing on the board was *Freshman Biology,* so we would know we were in the right place.

We filled the room. From whatever quirk of human nature it is, for our four years as biology majors, we would occupy, with almost no variation, the same seats we selected that first day.

The first order of business in my first class on my first day of college was a welcome from Dean Hightower. The freshman biology professor – Pearlman was his name, I think- was sifting through some papers and gave no indication anything would be starting soon, even though it was a few minutes into the hour. The murmurs of nervous chatter died down as Hightower entered.

"Is everyone here in the pre-medical program?" he started.

Dean Hightower looked his name. He had to be close to seven feet tall and had the build of a lineman. His skin was medium toned black, and his hair was clipped tight to his head. He spoke deliberately, striking the podium with his index finger for emphasis throughout his speech. Without the hair, he could have been Louis Gossett Jr. delivering the *Steers-and-Queers* speech from *An Officer and a Gentleman*. In a single motion he scanned the eyes of all in the room, registering the barely perceptible nods we offered to indicate that yes, we were all pre-med.

"Good. There are a few things I'm going to tell you that, until now, I'm willing to bet no one has ever told you. You all think you worked pretty hard to get here, and you did. We only accept about ten percent of the applications to our pre-medical program. You will be working much harder in college than you did in high school, and the only solace I offer you is that medical school will be that much harder. If that doesn't scare you, when and if you start your residency, you will work even harder and for more hours at a stretch than anyone in the world outside of the military. Then, when you finally get into the *real world*, most of you will be wishing you were back here in college."

Not exactly a pep talk. A few nervous laughs, then silence.

"Now, who chose medicine for the money?" He paused and slowly scanned the room.

A few hands went up tentatively – we were just out of high school and didn't know what we should keep to ourselves.

"You don't have to answer, Mr. Rensen," he said to a guy in the second row. "My questions this morning are rhetorical."

He knew our names.

"If you're in this for the money, you may want to reconsider. There are better ways to make money, and your colleagues in business school will have an eight-year head start on a six-figure salary. While they're driving past you in convertible Porsches, you'll be wondering if you can afford the car payments on your shit-box with your resident's salary and $100,000 student-loan debt. That's just the average; the less financially advantaged of you who go to the higher tuition medical schools can run up debts closer to $200,000. The good-life is deferred for a long time if you choose a career in medicine."

"I want to leave you with one last thought." He made a pyramid with his hands in front of his chest, like he was starting a prayer. "Make sure you all have a back-up plan."

I know it's only the psychos that think the TV or the newspaper is talking just to them, but I swear his eyes locked on me when he said we should have a back up plan.

"Look at the person to the left of you. Now look at the person to the right of you. Four years from now one of those people will not be going to medical school. It's my job to help you all get through, but from every class of one hundred fifty, only one hundred make it to the next level. I challenge you to break this tradition."

He put the phone numbers to the dean's office on the board. He was a full head taller than Pearlman, who had stood during Hightower's closing to set up the overheads for the first lecture.

Hightower said we should have a back-up plan. I should have had one then; I still don't have one now. I could have used one then.

I really need one now.

11

The parties at *Theta Theta Tau* weren't as wild as those in *Animal House*, but *Animal House's* were the target. The day before's personal invitation meant a lot, even after realizing the whole campus was invited. In addition to the door-to-door invitation extended to every freshman male, homemade signs advertising the party were nailed to everything on campus that would take a nail. It was called a Neutron Bomb party, and posters promised, like the bomb, that the only thing left standing would be the building. At the time, all-out nuclear war was still the social phobia – the cold war was still on, the Berlin Wall was still standing. I don't know what the change from the Cold War to the War on Terror has done for college party themes.

I made the ten-minute walk from my dorm room to the fraternity house alone. *"I want to be sedated..."* could be heard a few blocks away. The house was on the corner of Pine Street, and three doors down from the *Theta* house was an old guy waving and yelling from his porch. As it turned out, he would be out there before every party, and he would holler the same admonition at everyone who looked like they were heading to a party when they turned the corner.

"You tell those assholes to keep it down, or I'm calling the cops. Or maybe I'll just come over there with my rifle."

No rifle was ever produced. No cops ever came. We tried to soften him up by shoveling snow from his driveway or cleaning his yard in the spring and fall. It didn't do any good.

The fraternity house had a wraparound porch. A keg was set up in one corner, and a circle of girls wearing fraternity-letter shirts and smoking was in the other. There was a *No Smoking in the House* policy at *Theta Theta Tau,* and the only smoking inside was done in a room with a towel under the door and a fan in the window.

One of the brothers in a camouflage shirt and boxer shorts came over from the keg to greet me.

"How you doin'? I'm Francis."

"Hi. I'm Walter."

I put out my hand for a shake, but he snapped in a beer like he was passing me a track baton.

"Have a brew. Don't cost nothin'."

"Thanks."

The house was a late 1800's colonial, probably built by some wealthy family that did well in the post Civil War industrial boom of upstate New York. I'm sure they wouldn't have believed it if someone told them that their house would someday be home to forty college students who would get drunk in the living room, puke in the shower, get laid in the kids' bedrooms, and do all sorts of unmentionable things. The dining room was on the right as you entered and had a bar tended by two brothers in nothing but army helmets and camouflage boxer shorts. To the left was the living room, in the center of which was an oil drum labeled "radioactive punch." It was lit with black light and floated a block of dry ice that spewed fog. A large guy, who turned out to be the pledge master got in my face.

"Finish that!"

"Huh?"

"Chug!"

On his cue the dozen or so people who had been talking on the couches dropped their conversations and, in unison, began chanting, "Chug! Chug! Chug! Chug!"

I chugged.

"Wooooooooo!!!!" from the couches. Their conversations resumed.

The pledge master took a step back. He had put his eyes in line with my lips and the beer to make sure, like a referee might, that all the beer ended up where it was supposed to.

He gave a nod. "Thank you," he said. "Name's Bob."

I burped.

He clapped me on the back. "Have some punch."

I took some punch.

Vibrating through the floor was music and muffled shouts of, *"Hey…Hey what…Get laid, get fucked…"*

"There's a DJ downstairs. Catch you later." Bob tossed back his beer, filled his cup with punch, and went downstairs. I followed.

The basement floor was covered with sawdust. Billy Idol was still coming from the speakers chained to the corners of the ceiling. The centerpiece of the basement was a keg. There was a crowd around another bar to the right of the stairs, and there were several people dancing badly. The DJ was in a fraternity-letter shirt and wearing aviator sunglasses.

"What do you think?" a voice behind me said.

I turned around and saw the first truly beautiful girl I had seen since arriving at college. She was wearing a spaghetti-strap tank top and shorts set that showed off her large breasts and small hips She had long brown hair and big blue eyes.

The best I could come up with on short notice was, "It's nice."

"You wanna dance?"

I did not.

"Sure," I said. I downed my radioactive punch and she pulled me on the dance floor.

One of the worst things a dysrhythmic guy (like me) can do in public is dance. Watching someone else and trying to do what they do only puts you out of phase with the music and makes it worse. The liquor helped, if not my actual dancing, at least the sense that I wasn't doing too bad.

Ninety-nine Red Balloons came on and cleared the dance floor.

"Can you get me a drink?" she asked.

It was a tight squeeze at the basement bar, and the wait was long, but what could you expect with two twenty-year old English majors tending bar and free drinks.

"Hey, I saw you in class today," a guy I was jammed against said. "I'm Mike."

"Walter, Hi."

He was my height and thin with black hair and a short-sleeve checked shirt. He was holding hands with a girl who was standing behind him and looked as though she didn't want to be seen. He turned to reveal her.

"This is Donna, my girlfriend from home. She doesn't start school until next week, so she came up for the party."

"This is…" I smiled, pointing at my new friend. I didn't know her name.

"Mary. Hi," she said, not missing a beat.

"What's you're major?" Mike asked.

"I'm biology. Pre-med."

"Me too."

Mary squeezed my hand as though she was impressed. I thought about Kate for a moment. The moment passed.

Mike and I made small talk about where we were from, played an unsuccessful round of "Do you know…" and made our way to the bar. I got rum and Cokes for me and Mary, and I told Mike I'd see him later.

I took Mary up to the living room and we talked for a while. She was a local, said she worked at a convenience store in town. She told me she would show me around off-campus if I liked. We talked for an hour on one of the couches, adding beer and punch to the rum and Cokes. When she went to the bathroom, Bob the pledge master shook my hand, handing me a condom like he was passing a bribe to a maitre d' for a better table. I laughed and slid it in my pocket before Mary came back.

Cyndi Lauper's *Time After Time* came on and Mary jumped up. "I love this song. Lets go."

Back in the basement she put her arms around my neck, and we were dancing close – something you can do even if you don't have any rhythm. She kissed me quickly, looked in my eyes, then kissed me harder. As close as we were, I'm sure she could feel the stirring in my pants.

Bob appeared behind me and said in a low voice, but not whispering, "Room 23."

I broke the kiss, "Huh?"

"Room 23," Bob said. "Upstairs. Trust me."

I let Lauper go through one more chorus and asked Mary, "You want to go upstairs?"

She smiled and led me up by my hand. As we passed the living room, fraternity brothers watching us go upstairs made blowjob motions and humping gestures whenever they thought Mary wasn't looking.

"Where?" she asked.

"23." Room 23 could have been a toilet or a closet for all I knew, but up we went.

Room 23 was a small room with a twin-sized bunk bed on the far wall and a small desk on each of the short walls. An REM poster was the only wall decoration.

"It's nice. Is this your room?"

"No, I live on campus."

We stood facing each other for what seemed like forever. I figured I would screw it up somehow. I had nothing to say. Then, without warning, she took off her top. She had no bra. Her breasts were large and even with my limited experience seemed perfect, and I was drunk and I felt myself moving towards her.

We kissed for a while, standing. She had her hands on my hips, and as she started moving them towards the front of my pants, she paused at my pocket when she felt the crinkle of the condom wrapper. She reached in, pulled out Bob's condom and smiled.

She opened my fly and pushed my pants to the floor. I motioned with my eyes towards the top bunk and she nodded. She took off her shorts revealing black panties, and climbed the ladder. I watched her as she disappeared under a blanket. I climbed the ladder to join her.

I kissed her breasts and she rolled on top of me. I fumbled around the sheets trying to feel for where she had left the condom. There was a knock at the door.

I ignored it.

Another knock.

I ignored it again.

A third knock.

"Busy!" I yelled.

"It's important." It sounded like Mike, the guy with the girlfriend from the basement.

"Can't it wait?"

"It shouldn't."

"Uhmm...Mary?" I said.

"Go see. But hurry."

I opened the door.

Mike looked through the crack in the door first at my face and then at my crotch. "Number five, huh," he said,

I started college with a new six-pack of tighty-whities, and stuck on my underpants, where my penis was trying to poke through, was a sticker suggesting my erection had been "Inspected by No. 5."

In a whisper Mike said, "Do what you want, but the guys downstairs are saying Mary is fifteen and that her father is a local judge."

"You're shitting me."

"I just thought you would want to know. Statutory rape is a bad way to start college."

"Thanks. Thanks a lot." I had been deflating since he said the word rape and my No. 5 sticker fell to the ground.

"Mary. I'm sorry. I gotta go."

She sat up, looking confused. The blanket slid down and revealed her left breast. I shook my head to clear it like Wille E. Coyote would after Road Runner hit him on the head with an anvil. I went downstairs and headed for the keg.

The hallways of the house were lined with composite photos of head and shoulders shots of all of the brothers who lived in the fraternity house in past years. The people in the photos would have been eighteen to twenty-two years old at the time of the pictures, but I was struck by how all of the photos from the 50's and early 60's looked like they could have been my father. They, too, were all eighteen to twenty-two then, but they all looked like middle-aged men, all with crew cuts and thick glasses. Something bad happened to the hairstyles in the late sixties and seventies. The photos from the early eighties all looked like they were of college kids. The transition from year to year was subtle but undeniable – the same-aged students looked less mature as time went on. I paused to contemplate this until I was overcome with the urge to piss.

Bob blocked the entrance to the living room on my return. He pointed one thumb up and one thumb down, and pumped his eyebrows waiting for me to indicate how things had gone with Mary.

I paused, then showed a thumbs down.

"Survey says...!" he shouted in the manner of Richard Dawson on *Family Feud*.

A chorus on the couch crossed their forearms in an "X" while mimicking the game show's buzzer indicating an incorrect answer.

I downed another glass of punch – there was only a sputtering speck of dry ice left in the punch bowl. I filled another glass for the road and started towards my dorm.

On my drunken walk home, I tripped a few times, took a leak off an overpass, and puked in the woods. After I made it home, I remember thinking how I would like join *Theta Theta Tau*.

12

The evening after we received our bids, twenty freshmen, including myself, met in the living room of *Theta Theta Tau*. Most of us figured we would receive the bids; there were a few people not there who said they would join if invited, so they must not have received bids. There were four people not present that I knew were asked to join, so they must have elected either to not go Greek or to join another house. Bob the pledge master made some welcoming remarks to let us know how lucky we were to have the opportunity to pledge the Ts and how not everyone that wanted to join was afforded the opportunity. We considered ourselves lucky. The mood was light. There was lots of laughter at off-color jokes that would be the mainstay of fraternity conversation for the three years I would live in the house. The first snap into seriousness came with a question from John Packer.

"Do we have to live in the frat after we become brothers?" John asked.

Bob stood, turned his back to us, looked up at the ceiling and paused before speaking.

"John," he said, "Do you call your mother a moth?"

"Uh...no."

"Would you call your country a cunt?"

"No."

"You are in a fraternity. A FRA-TER-NI-TY. Not a frat. A fraternity."

After I was initiated a brother in *Theta Theta Tau*, I often repeated that reasoning to the newest batch of freshmen. I'm not sure why, but it seemed important at the time.

A tour of the house followed. We saw each brother's room and were expected to remember whose room was whose. We were shown the house phone. Whenever a pledge was in the house, they were expected to answer the common phone on three rings or less with, "Thank you for calling *Theta Theta Tau,* the best and strongest fraternity at Midstate, how can I direct your call?" I'm sure the callers on the other end were as annoyed with the phone speech as you are at a donut shop drive-thru listening to the speaker-voice rattle off a list of specials when all you want is a coffee.

The last stop of the fraternity tour was the library. The library was suspiciously named, for there were no books. The only furniture in the room was filing cabinets, four cabinets along one wall and three more between the windows. Each draw was labeled with a range of five-digit numbers.

"These are our test files," Bob said. "Unless a new professor comes in, these files contain every test from every semester from just about every course. We have had brothers in all major programs and have collected hundreds of exams. The last thing professors give a shit about is teaching and testing undergraduates. Professors are here to write papers and get grants – that's how their success is measured. Teaching is an interruption. They almost never make up new exams. They repeat tests at least every three years. Some of them- look at Psych 101 – give the same test every year. There's a school policy against test files, but nobody asks, and nobody talks about them- most fraternities keep them."

I remember thinking how cool that was. The dean was telling us how it was time to start the hard work and how a third of us wouldn't make it through to medical school. Here was an insurance policy. I could read the thousand-page text to get ready for a test, or I could spend a couple hours in the fraternity library and see all the questions beforehand. The exams determined the grades. It turned out those files had back-tests on better than 4 out of 5 classes I took each semester. It wouldn't guarantee I'd get into medical school, but it would make sure my GPA was high enough.

After the tour we were given our pledge pins and were told we had to wear them anytime we had a shirt on until after Hell Week. A few of us asked what Hell Week was all about. Bob's answer turned out to be accurate not just for Hell Week, but for most of life's difficult times:

"Hell Week is the best week of your life to look back on."

After that first of what would be weekly pledge meetings, several kegs were tapped. I funneled my first beer, played my first game of quarters, puked in the backyard, and passed out in the dining room.

Good times.

13

Attached to my Biophysiology mid-term was a note from the professor:

Dear Mr. Most –
Please call my secretary to set up an appointment to discuss your performance in my class.
– Prof. Underwood

I figured I was busted. Thanks to the test files, I got 100% on the mid-term, a score that had never been achieved in the ten years Underwood had taught the 101 Biophysiology course. I figured I was going to get in some kind of trouble for cheating, or someone had tipped him off to the fraternity's test files. Almost one-third the school went Greek, and most of the houses had some kind of test files, and Underwood's tests looked like they repeated every three years, so a lot of people must have done pretty well on the test. It *was* a 200-question test. I suppose even if you've seen the questions before, with that many questions, you're bound to get something wrong. Either that, or the others, smarter than me, threw a few questions to not make it so obvious they had seen the questions before taking the test.

"I'm Walter Most. I'm here to see Professor Underwood."

"Right this way," his secretary got up from her desk and led me down the hall. The secretary was stationed in a small room at the top of the stairs of the third floor of the Old Research Building. There were no elevators. There were closed doors at the end of the halls on each side that led away from her office, and she had to use a key to get us through.

I asked why the doors were locked. She told me that every so often the animal rights people acted up and pulled stunts to make it harder for the animal research to go on. When they were active, they would stage protests or do things like let the air out of the tires of the animal delivery trucks- anything to interfere with the running of the labs. The year before she started, a nighttime raid freed all the animals from their cages. When people arrived the next morning, there were rats running loose, pigs with intravenous lines eating out of garbage cans, and cocaine addicted monkeys tearing the place apart looking for a fix. It was the reason her predecessor had quit. In the seventies, one of the professors was duct taped and left naked in a chicken wire cage for the weekend with nothing but lab chow, water bottles, and a pile of cedar chips to relieve himself on. It took him a couple of month to recover mentally, but eventually he got back to work, and the research continued.

When she opened the door separating her office from Underwood's lab, I was struck with a smell that was a combination of cedar chips and a bus-terminal men's room. "You'll get used to it," she told me that first day. The lab was on the top floor, and the ceiling tiles had water spots from places where the roof had leaked. The cinder block walls were painted tan and had no decorations, save the occasional OSHA bulletin or lab safety update taped to the wall. The color of the wall had previously been a sky blue that could be seen poking through where the tan paint had been removed along with the tape holding up an outdated bulletin or safety update.

Underwood's secretary said *I would get used to it*. I remember doing a double-take when she said that. It was as though she expected me to be back, and not once, but regularly. My belief on being called to see Underwood was that I was in some kind of trouble. Also, if I was being invited to something, it was a little presumptive to assume I would be willing. As I would find out, nobody had ever refused Professor Underwood, and I wouldn't be the first.

His office was small, perhaps eight by six, and just passed the locked door. There was a poster over the window of a baby with a bowl of spaghetti turned over his head, *"I'm having one of those days"* in block letters below the baby's crying face. There was a signed baseball under glass on a shelf over his desk, and besides his college issue brown metal desk, brown metal filing cabinet, and his office chair, there were no other furnishings. There were papers everywhere. Some were graph paper pages with diagrams of apparatus sketched on them. Some papers stuck out from between the pages of notebooks. There was no apparent system of organization, except that perhaps what had been worked on most recently would be closer to the top of any given pile.

"Mr. Most, come in," Underwood said, without looking up from his desk.

"Hello, Professor."

"Do you know why you're here?" he asked.

Underwood had thinning black and gray hair and a full beard. He had an academic appearance that was emphasized by a tobacco pipe that he was always handling but rarely smoked.

"No, sir." I'm usually not that formal, but I was still pretty sure I was about to be busted for cheating or some code of ethics violation because of the test files. My standing and his sitting added to the inquest feeling. I'm not sure why I thought that maintaining a "No, I haven't been drinking, officer," tone might have helped me at the time, but it's the tone I used.

"Every year I invite an undergraduate to assist me in the lab with my research," he began. "It's a good experience. I invite those who show the most promise, and your perfect test score, the first in my recollection, makes you a good candidate. Have you thought about doing research as an undergrad?"

I couldn't believe it. I didn't know shit about his course except for the answers to a test to which I had already seen the questions. Some research experience *would* help me get into medical school, I knew that. As I saw it then, it didn't matter how I earned the privilege of being invited into Underwood's lab, it was the results that counted.

"Yes, I would be interested."

"You're pre-med, right?"

"Yes, sir."

"Enough with the sir. I'm Frank. Call me Frank, or Dr. Underwood if you need to, but save your *sirs* for someone else. Okay? Okay."

"What would I be doing?"

"Lab assistant work. Weighing and feeding the animals. Administering study medications. Euthanasia at the end of the studies. My graduate students run the individual studies. Let's go to the lab and I'll introduce you. They can show you what we do here, and if you're still interested, welcome aboard."

He led me further down the hall to another set of doors that were also locked. He turned the key and swung the doors open, revealing a man with red hair and a goatee at the top of an eight-foot ladder and a shorter man with a crew cut standing at the bottom. They both turned their heads towards us when we opened the door, causing the guy at the bottom to miss the rat that had just been dropped by the guy at the top. The rat hit the linoleum with a thud, shook it off, and took to running circles around the lab.

"Shit, Frank, you really should knock first," the guy at the bottom said. "We're breaking in a new batch."

"Sorry," Underwood wasn't. "This is Walter Most. He's a freshman, and I've offered him the opportunity to join our lab as an assistant this year."

"Hey Walter, Steve," from the top of the ladder.

"Martin," from the guy at the bottom.

Steve took another rat from the box he had at the top of the ladder, tossed it underhand towards the ceiling, then followed it with his eyes as it ascended, peaked and then descended, all the while the rat spinning its front and back legs in wild circles. The rat landed in the work-gloved hands of Martin at the bottom with a muffled catcher's mitt sound. Martin stroked the rat's back, talked baby talk to it, then brought it to a steel cage. He got back into position for the next rodent. Dr. Underwood had left.

"What are you doing?" I asked.

Steve, from the top, "We're breaking them in."

Martin, from the bottom, "We're getting them used to being handled. We just got a new shipment of lab rats today. Steve's wearing a chain-mail glove up there. He freaks them out by tossing them through the air. I catch them and treat them nice with these leather lab gloves that we use during the experiments. It makes them feel comfortable when they're held in these gloves, so they'll cooperate with us during the protocols. We just have a few left. Take a look around."

I walked around the lab. There were several steel frames, each with thirty-six small cages. Each cage housed one rat. The rats came up to the front when I poked my head in their cages to check them out. There was one rack of cages where the rats looked like they had been fitted with plastic backpacks. There were tubes that came out of the backpacks and tunneled under the rats' skin. There were water bottles of different colors arranged in a non-accidental pattern, suggesting it was for some scientific reason. In the back of the lab was a large habitrail set-up with a large rat running on the wheel. The rat was at least three times the size of the rats that were playing catch with Steve and Martin, and its hair was a bit yellowed with age, not pure white like the rats being taken from the cardboard box at the top of the ladder. Over the habitrail was a Sports Illustrated calendar open to April of the previous year - the calendar was years out of date - displaying Paulina Porizkova. Over the calendar on track-feed computer paper was a banner reading "TEMPLE OF PAULINA."

The rat running on the wheel in the "temple" was larger, older, and wiser appearing than the other rats. She also had a tail of many colors. Her tail was painted with rings of purple, red, blue, yellow, and pink. Some of the colors were bright and vibrant, some of them had faded to almost nothing.

"What's with this one?" I asked.

"That's Paulina," said Steve.

"We worship Paulina," said Martin.

"The model or the rat?"

"Both, really."

Steve came down the ladder. "You've been to Europe?"

I shook my head "no".

"How 'bout China?"

"No."

"Well Paulina has been around the world."

"The model or the rat?"

"Um, again, both. We did an experiment a couple of years ago that required a bunch of special analysis. One test had to be done in Germany, one in China, and one in California. The rats had to be alive at the time of blood and tissue biopsy, so we needed to send them around the world. We needed a way to code the rats so we could send them from place to place and tell which was which. We tested the color code on Paulina. She made a six-day FedEx trip around the world. When she got back, we saw which colors survived the transit and used those in the experiment. She wasn't assigned into an experimental group and was thus spared. Now she is our lab mascot. She's outlived the average rat's life expectancy by two years."

Steve showed me around the rest of the lab. Most of the experiments had to do with the effects of illegal drugs – amphetamine, cocaine, marijuana- on vital organs. Underwood became famous several years earlier by developing an assay that could detect subtle changes in liver, kidney, and brain chemistry in living test subjects. Probes with fine pipets were surgically implanted into the rats, and fluid could be removed for analysis or various microprobes could be placed for measurement or stimulus.

The research funding was coming mostly from drug companies, but earlier in Underwood's career most of the funding came from the government. The "Just Say No" campaign put tons of government money into drug abuse prevention and treatment research, although anyone working in the field would have told you that government-funded research would never make a dent in the problem. This futility did not prevent drug abuse research from becoming a sure way to grow a well-funded lab.

"I try to give an undergraduate the opportunity to participate in our lab each year," Underwood had reappeared at the door while we were paying homage to Paulina (the rat). "Generally, it is a lot of grunt work. The rats need to be weighed and fed every day, including weekends. When there are medications to administer, we have to prepare up to 100 injections at a time. At the beginning of a project there is often some minor surgery. At the end of the experiments, the rats are sacrificed. My graduate students perform most of the data analysis, and you are welcome to participate in the writing of the research paper to the extent you are able to and are interested. What do you think?"

I couldn't think of any reason to refuse. I would get the chance to do some research, which would look good on my medical school applications. Underwood knew it was a great opportunity.

I told Underwood I would join his lab – it was better than the suspension or expulsion I was convinced was the reason for his wanting to see me in he first place.

That was the day my research career began. As you may have figured out by now, I never made it to medical school. How things might have turned out differently if I had just gone to medical school, God only knows. Or, as Steve and Martin would have said, "Only Paulina knows."

14

I was not alone when Kate called. Lisa, this girl I had started seeing from the Beta sorority, was still in bed with me from the night before. Lisa and I hooked up after a party before spring break. We got drunk and wound up sleeping with each other that night, and since that night, we ended up in bed together about once a week. Before that first time, and before each of our weekly sessions, she would make a point of reminding me that she had a boyfriend back home, and that each time we were together would likely be the last. Lisa had been my first. I told her there had been others, and I guess I did okay because she never called bullshit on my claims of experience, and she came back to my room each week. The sex got more intense each time– one of the guys at the fraternity told me there was nothing quite like a farewell fuck. There might be something to that, even if with Lisa it was always a false farewell. When the phone rang, Lisa and I had just finished an AM romp that followed a drunken session the night before.

I rolled on my back to answer the phone. The last cool drops trickled down the outside of my thigh and onto Lisa.

I had seen Kate over Thanksgiving and winter break, and we talked on the phone about every other week. I think we both knew if there wasn't the distance between us, the situation might have been different. If we weren't so far apart we could have tried to make it work– I would have been an idiot for not trying if there was any chance. She had hinted, although never said, that she had met someone at her school. I didn't bother going home for spring break - I stayed in town and waited tables at a diner for some extra cash.

Lisa grabbed a towel for her leg as I answered the phone.

"Kate." I recognized her voice on contact. "Hi."

"Hi, Walter, how are you doing?"

"Good. Good."

"Are you alone?"

I'm sure she could tell I wasn't.

"Yes." Good answer.

"Walter, I can get out of here next weekend. I'd like to come and see you."

"That would be...good."

"You sure?"

"Yes."

"You really alone?"

Lisa threw the towel in the corner and started looking for her clothes.

"Yes! Next weekend is good."

"O.K. See you."

"Bye, now."

She had to know I wasn't alone. What an asshole I was. She couldn't expect me to sit around for four years waiting for her, could she? She was seeing somebody in Maine, wasn't she?

"Who was that?" Lisa's voice shocked me back to college from high school.

"A friend from back home. He wants to come up this weekend."

"He?" she smiled.

"Uh...yeah, from high school."

"Hey, this weekend some of our sorority is road tripping to Canada, so I won't be around anyway. Just don't catch anything."

"What do you mean?"

"If you want to screw your "he" friend next weekend, go ahead. I told you, this is probably our last time together. I have a boyfriend, you know."

"I know. You said that last week. And the week before."

"But this time I mean it."

"You said that last time too."

She sat on the edge of my bed and put on her bra.

"Well I hope you enjoyed it this morning, because this really was our last time."

"I did, thank you."

"Thank you? Thank you?! You get your rocks off and say "thank you" like I just handed you the morning paper? Asshole. Have fun with your friend next weekend."

"I'm sorry. I didn't mean it like that. I really enjoyed..." I waved my arms over my bed, "this. I'm sorry it has to end."

"That's better. I had fun, too."

She put on her panties. She looked at me with mischievous eyes.

"Umm..." she said. "Seeing how this is our last time together, you wanna go one more time?" She opened the front clasps of her bra but held the cups in place with her hands.

I thought of Kate. I needed to keep clean thoughts for Kate. Kate could be the one. Kate. But there was Lisa. She was hot, horny, and most important at the time, she was right there. And she had her hands on her undone bra. How could I leave her standing there like that?

"I can't," I said somehow. "I have to go take care of the rats."

15

I told Kate to meet me at the lab on Saturday. I figured since it was my weekend to feed and weigh the rats, I'd get it out of the way before she arrived, and, since it was the first time she would be coming to see me at college, I'd make myself look important by having her see me doing some important research. I spent the morning going over how I looked, changing my clothes a few times. I thought about wearing one of those white lab coats – the kind you see in commercials where everyone is trying to look scientific – but that would have been stupid. I told her to call me from the campus phone in the foyer of the research building so I could get her through the security doors.

"Hi," she said, kissing me on the cheek. She caught me off guard and I kissed the air.

"You look great," I said. She did. "Come up, I'm almost finished."

I could have been finished, but I saved the last few rats so there would be something for her to watch me do. She followed me up the stairs and took my hand after I unlocked the door to the lab.

"This is pretty cool," she said as she looked around the lab. "How'd you get involved in all this? I don't remember you being interested in research."

"I guess things change. I took Professor Underwood's class and did well. I expressed interest, and he offered me a spot in his lab."

I exaggerated a little. I just wanted it to sound better than, "I cheated on his test, and now I'm trying to pad my resume for medical school applications."

"I haven't done anything like this at my school," she said. "I'm just doing what I can to get by."

"Come on. What did you get last semester, a 4.0 or something."

"No. 3.8. But I have to work really hard and the classes aren't getting easier. How'd you do?"

"I got a 3.2. Not great, but hopefully good enough for medical school. I got an A in Underwood's class and a B in everything else. But I'm having a good time. It's been great pledging *Theta Theta Tau*. Hell Week is coming up soon."

"The frat sounds cool. When can I see it?"

"We'll go by the house tonight. There's a continuous keg at eight." I wasn't going to offer the 'frat' speech.

"What's a continuous keg?"

"You'll see. It's unnecessary, but fun. They do it every Saturday."

I finished the last rat and then introduced Kate to Paulina.

"You want to hold her."

"Sure. What's with the calendar?"

"The grad students who work here think Paulina is hot, and since the rat is named after her, they thought it would be a nice way to decorate."

"What do you think of her?" she asked.

"The rat or the model?"

"The model."

"She's okay."

"Just okay? How could you say she's not hot?"

"You didn't come here this weekend to tell me you've switched sides, have you?" I said.

"Because I think Paulina looks hot in a bathing suit? Like you think I don't think that's what you think?"

"They say 50 percent of girls in college do some experimentation in college, you know."

"They also say 90% of guys act like idiots in college, you know."

"Sorry," I said. "I'm trying too hard. You're all I've been thinking about since you called. I'm very happy you came up. I don't mean to be a jerk. I'm sorry."

She stopped stroking Paulina's back and took my hand. Kate and both Paulinas were now staring at me. Paulina the rat was freaking me out – she looked like she understood what was going on. I shuddered when Kate started talking again – for a second it felt like her voice was coming from the rat.

"That's better," she said. "I wanted to see you."

She came in close, and I kissed her. Too close; the rat squeaked from the pressure.

"I guess we should put Paulina back," she said, kissing the rat. "Bye, baby."

She set the rat back in her cage. The animal was completely at ease. Kate would have laughed at me if she was in the lab my first few days. I was scared of the rats, and the rats were scared of me.

"Let me show you around campus," I said, leading her out of the lab.

I slipped my arm around Kate's waist. Walking close with her was comfortable. We talked about our new lives and what we missed and didn't miss from home. We had dinner at a pizza pub in town; the other tables turned over two or three times while we talked, ignoring the waitresses who kept asking if they could get us anything else. When we were finished it was still warm enough to walk up to the house. We got to *Theta Theta Tau* as they were tapping the keg.

"So what's a continuous keg?" She asked over the cheering crowd in the living room.

Bob appeared and looked Kate up and down. "Nice, Walter," he said, "Very nice."

"That's the pledge master – he's like that. Sorry"

"You don't have to apologize for your friends."

"Tell me that after you've seen them drunk."

"Are we supposed to get in line?" she asked.

"That's the continuous keg. There are a hundred-something beers in a keg. The only rule is that once the tap is opened, it doesn't shut. You line up, get a beer, and go to the end of the line. You're beer needs to be finished by the time you get to the front again. We win when the keg is drained."

"What if you lose?"

"I don't know. I've never seen that happen, but I imagine it's not pretty."

The keg went according to form. The line started with about 20, Kate and I were at the end, so it took a couple of minutes to get our cups filled. I told her if she wanted to do it right, she'd have to chug it down pretty quick. After two fills some of the lightweights dropped out, and the third lap went quicker. Some of the guiltier-feeling brothers who had dropped out ran through the house recruiting those still in their rooms to partake so the keg wouldn't need to be shut down. Kate was keeping up. In less than a year at school we had built up an enormous tolerance, not just for the alcohol, but also for the volume.

We filled our fourth, and Kate made a face that said she'd have to sit the next lap out. I joined her on the couch.

"This is stupid," Kate said. She burped, then laughed.

"Don't let us down, Walter." Bob was in my face again. "It's almost drained."

Kate burped again, shook her head at me to exclude herself, but said with some urgency, "They need you, Walter. Get in there."

At least I got to skip one round. Some drunken math told me the keg must die soon, but the gold fluid kept flowing.

Soon it was just me, Bob, Francis, and some guy I didn't know. I was one away from the tap, and my sixth was barely touched. Each sip crawled towards my stomach, threatening to come back up. One more beer and I would boot for sure.

It became like one of those slow-motion scenes from a baseball movie: the kind with a ninth inning game-saving catch. I saw Fred's beer almost full at the tap, Bob motioning me to get ready. Louder than the alcohol-muffled shouts was the rumbling of the beer in my belly.

Bob motioned me to the keg, his arms flailing wildly like he was waving me home from third. "W-a-l-t-e-r---N-o-w!!!!"

Then it appeared. A plastic cup eased Fred's off the tap and accepted the flow. Kate had saved me. Her cup filled halfway when the keg spewed the foam that signaled its demise. It was dry. Bob took Kate's free hand and raised it over her head, cheering like we had won something important.

"She saved your ass," Bob said. "Love this girl, or someone else will."

He was right.

"Strong work," Bob said to Kate. "Where'd you learn to drink like that?"

"You don't know you have some talents until you try," she said, then burped and laughed again.

I was pretty lit. I was watching Kate's mouth move, seeing the words come out more than hearing them.

"Show me the rest of the house," she said.

I took her hand and we stumbled around the house, laughing as we tripped down the halls, me introducing her to anyone we came across.

"Who lives there?" she asked, pointing at Room 23.

"Nobody. That's a spare room they use for..."

"What?"

"Nothing."

She could tell from my blush what "nothing" meant. She could read my mind. I felt the heat in my cheeks.

"Come on," she said, leading me towards Room 23.

"Really?"

"Ask me again, and I might change my mind."

I was drunk, and she was drunk. I had enough of my mind left to know what was happening, though. She led me into Room 23. I shut the door behind us. She climbed the ladder of the bunk bed.

"You want to be on top?" I asked.

"A bit presumptive aren't you?"

"I mean on top of the bed. The top bunk of the bed."

"I'm up here, aren't I?"

I climbed the ladder – the first two steps anyway. I stumbled and struck my face on the top rung. My nose started bleeding.

"I'm just not lucky in this bed," I muttered, thinking back to the judge's daughter and not thinking how bad that must have sounded.

"What's that?" she said.

"I wish I hadn't hit my head," a nice drunken cover. It would be a bad time to tell Kate the story of the 15-year-old I brought here just a few months earlier. She let it go.

"Get up here. Let me see your face. It's not too bad."

I wiped the blood off my face with the bottom of my shirt. The bleeding had stopped. I was sure there would be swelling.

She kissed the top of my nose, then my cheeks, then my face, then our tongues found each other, and I put my arms around her back.

"I've missed you," she said.

She sat up, her head just clearing the ceiling, and she opened her shirt. She looked down toward her chest and gave a subtle nod. I opened the clasps of her bra. The summer after high school, I saw her in some pretty small bikinis, but I always fantasized about what she would look like with no clothes on. There was no doubt she wouldn't be fantastic, but fantasies typically disappoint when they come true. Not this time.

I pulled her in towards me. We kissed, then kissed harder. I felt her pull at the button of my jeans and undo the zipper. I had on boxers, and my penis popped out through the fly when she lowered my pants. She laughed.

"It's not nice to laugh at it."

"Sorry. It looked like it was trying to bust out on its own."

"It was."

She pulled down my boxers, snagging the waistband on my erection. She laughed again.

"Are you going to keep laughing at it?"

She leaned back and eased her pants and panties off in one motion. Then she rolled on top of me.

"You asked if I wanted to be on top," she said.

She wriggled around to find me and used her hand to guide me in the right direction. My mind faded black as I shut my eyes, and the only awareness I had was of my entering her.

16

"It's quicker if you inject them here," Steve said as he slid the needle into the rat's abdomen.

The rat squirmed on contact with the needle, but then settled. It had received daily injections for the past month as part of the study protocol. To the rat, this one was no different.

"You have to move fast," Steve continued. "At some point, the rats at the bottom of the rack figure out what's going on and start flipping out."

I had never intentionally killed an animal. Well, I've fished, so I guess I'll change that to I've never intentionally killed a mammal. I've creamed my share of squirrels on the road, but they were accidents. This was different; this was killing. Or, as Steve and Martin put it, euthanizing.

The data collection was complete, and the animals would be put down. The study protocol included autopsies to confirm the location of the surgical catheters we had placed at the beginning of the project, as well as tissue sampling to check for any kidney or liver damage. The rats would die so that others (people, that is) might live, or at least might live better.

I took the pre-loaded 60 cc syringe, put on a lab glove and picked up my first rat. Steve started at the top, I started at the bottom. We would meet in the middle. Three ccs were required to put each rat to sleep and stop its breathing. One syringe could bump-off twenty rats. I jabbed #36 and pushed the plunger to the prescribed line. The rat was moving noticeably slower when I shut his cage.

The rats in the middle row started to look nervous. They were rearing up on their hind legs. Two were spinning circles; two looked like they were tap dancing. I don't know how they communicated with each other that something was up, especially as they were dying. The procedure was essentially the same as it was on the days the rats received study injections, and they never acted like this before, so they must have been able to pass on the information somehow that they were about to die.

"Mother-fucker!"

Steve had been bitten through his glove. The rat was dangling from his gloved hand and spinning like a disco ball.

"Grab him."

I put my glove around the rat's chest and squeezed. Steve pulled down its tail and hit it in the abdomen with his syringe. He put the syringe down, grabbed the rat from my hand, and tossed it roughly in its cage.

"Bastard."

"You all right?"

"Yeah, that happens sometimes."

"Rabies?"

"Rats don't carry rabies," Steve said. "Unless we got bats in the lab, there's no way for them to even be exposed."

"What now?"

"The necks."

"What do you mean?"

"Now we have to snap their necks. The drugs work, but they don't always kill them all the way. You got to take them like this..." he picked up rat number one and held it in a ring formed by his thumb and index finger. "Then you twist their heads around 180 degrees... You'll feel a pop when you get there."

I heard the pop. The now twice-dead rat was limp in his hand with its head at a disturbing angle. He put it in a black plastic garbage bag and picked up the next one.

"Go ahead," he said.

I didn't like the feeling in my hands as the first rat's neck snapped. It felt and sounded like cracking your knuckles under water. I kept going, but only at a pace of six rats to Steve's twelve.

"When do they get the autopsy?" I asked.

"We don't always do that. It takes too long, and the tissue samples are too expensive to run. We'll do autopsies on a few of them if we are testing new compounds or using a new surgical technique, but Underwood's been doing this for a long time; he doesn't always do the autopsies."

"Don't the papers say the rats have autopsies and tissue samples?"

"That has to be in there so the papers will get published. We've reconciled that by talking about what rats in our lab *have* received, without necessarily implying it was what we did with the rats in the current study- check it out."

"Is that legit?"

"Not entirely, but it's how things are done," Steve was not interested in explaining it much further. "We all know how the autopsies come out, so why bother. And the drug companies can do their own tissue studies if it turns out the drugs work at all."

I've since looked at some of Underwood's older publications; it was true. The protocols generally read: The rats were injected with compound X on days 1,3,5 and 7 of the study period. Half of the rats received placebo injections...Rats were autopsied to confirm the location of the catheters and assess for tissue damage.

Apparently, referring to the autopsied rats as "rats" and not "the studied rats" allowed some leeway into the interpretation and could mean rats in general had been autopsied for catheter location and tissue damage, which at some time, some rats had been, but that "these rats" used in the experiment were not necessarily "those rats." It wasn't honest, but it wasn't my lab. I did what they told me.

"Cover me," Steve said, "I'm going to make a withdrawal."

THC, the active ingredient in marijuana, is highly volatile. In its purified form it has to be stored in dark glass under oil, or it will degrade or evaporate. Even though pot is illegal, the company for which Underwood was doing research wanted to know if there was any possible interaction between the drug they were developing to treat depression and pot. Since so many depressed people smoked regularly, it was likely that the two drugs would be present in some of the people some of the time. A drop of the pure stuff taken orally would get you as high as an entire night's smoking.

The withdrawal method was simple. Steve kept a sample bottle of olive oil in his backpack. He would go into the stock-locker and exchange a few drops of the THC for a few drops of distilled water, then he'd put the stolen THC into his oil bottle for use at home. The fill-level of the bottle never changed, and, if analyzed, the stock-bottle would always come back full of THC – Steve never altered the concentration too much. Underwood rarely came into the lab by surprise, but Steve always asked me to watch the door so he wouldn't get caught with his hands in the cookie jar.

I wrote the methods section for that, my first paper. I basically copied the methods section from Underwood's prior studies, substituting the drugs used and the injection protocols to match the experiment we were working on. I included the statements about the autopsies, even though I knew we hadn't done any autopsies. It was how they did things.

"Nice work on the paper," Underwood said to me a few weeks later as we were sending it off to a publisher. "If you decide to get your master's instead of going to medical school, we can probably make some room for you here."

"Thank you," I said.

It bothered me that Underwood would intentionally submit a misleading paper. He was supposed to be this hot-shot researcher with a national reputation- he even had a technique named after him - but he cut corners to save some time and money and didn't report what he did. How much of his "important" work had been done like that?

Every so often there is some article in the paper or some story on CNN that exposes some dishonest scientist caught falsifying data. Recently, a few reports that were thought of as important breakthroughs needed to be retracted because of *technical errors* discovered after publication. I'm sure some of the problems with the reports turned out to be fabrications, not just errors. I've seen it happen before. You think what you're making up for publication is insignificant, but then it gets picked up by the media for some reason, and now your exaggerated science is "out there" for all to see. First it's flattering, then it's embarrassing.

I know. After what I've done who cares what I think about scientific honesty? But I'm telling you, I'm not the only one – it might be the honest types who turn out to be the exceptions.

17

Hell Week is a bit of a blur, but, just like they had said, it's a good week to look back on. With barely enough time left in freshman year to cram for finals, I was initiated a brother in *Theta Theta Tau*. The secret rituals weren't as earth shattering as I would have guessed, but what makes them special is that they were, and are, secret.

The sleep deprivation of Hell Week and the weekend long party that followed got me past any residual guilt I felt about what I had written for Underwood, and lessened the disappointment I harbored in Underwood's research ethics. Steve and Martin told me about a new project they were starting, and I agreed to help.

I was looking at between a 2.5 and a 3.0 for the second semester. With a C locked in for both organic chemistry and calculus – locked in is the unfortunate circumstance of there being no reasonable final exam performance that could influence your grade one way or another – I'd have to crank on my other finals to keep my 3.0 average, the lowest GPA that might be acceptable to medical schools. With a PhD and not an MD after my name, you know how it worked out in the end. As it turned out, my contribution to the pre-med program was to be someone else's guy on the left or right who wouldn't be going to medical school. To whomever got my spot: you're welcome.

Since we had been together, I had been talking to Kate on the phone more – about twice a week. I had renewed optimism about a long-distance relationship. The distance was still a problem, but maybe we could work something out.

The weekend after Kate came up, I managed to avoid Lisa, but she appeared the following Friday, and we picked up where we left off. Each time was still to be the last. Lisa knew about Kate and didn't care. To Lisa I was just a place keeper while she was away at school. She believed she loved her boyfriend, and she probably did. She talked about him all the time, and I think her talking about him got her all hot, and there I was. She couldn't help it, and, at least before Kate was back in my life, I didn't mind.

Lisa came over the Sunday after we were initiated into Theta Theta Tau. She had seen us pledges during Hell Week, performing stupid stunts in the quad. Even though we weren't supposed to have any female contact for the duration of Hell Week, she came over to me while I was holding a fishing pole over a sewer to tell me she would come over after we were finished. I had been initiated a brother, and we had just had sex in the shower. I wish she had never come over.

"I won't be seeing you before finals," she said, "I'm going home to see my boyfriend."

"Why are you going now?" I asked. "The semester ends in two weeks."

"I just need to see him. Besides, you said you needed to study more."

"I should, but I don't think I can move my grades that much either way."

"You're going to do better than me," she said. "I'll be lucky if I get Cs."

"Yeah, but I need better than a 3.0 if I'm going to go to medical school."

There was a knock at the door.

"Go away!" I yelled.

Another knock.

"Not now!"

Another knock.

"I'm studying!"

"I thought you might like a break."

I felt the blood rushing from my head and chest as I recognized the voice. I was still wet from the shower, but I felt myself start to sweat.

"Get dressed!" I said to Lisa.

I put on some shorts and an inside out t-shirt. I was trying to think of ways to talk myself out of the situation that was about to present itself. I could pull out some report I was working on, put some paper in the typewriter, and have Lisa look like she was dictating something for me to type. I could get out some books and say we were studying – it was 10AM on a Sunday, but it could have been the case. I had three reasonable (at least to me) excuses set to go as I went to the door.

I opened the door slowly and watched Kate's face change from hopeful to horrified when her eyes went from me to Lisa. I started to deliver excuse number 2, but what came out was, "I'm sorry. It's not what you think."

"I think it is what I think. And I think you're an asshole."

She ran off. She never looked back as I chased her down the hall and out to the parking lot. She drove off.

"Fuck," I said when I got back to my room. Lisa was getting her stuff together.

"I'm sorry," Lisa said.

"You didn't do anything. Fuck."

"You gonna be okay?"

"Yeah, I'll straighten things out with her."

"I'll see you after break, okay."

"Yeah. Have fun with your boyfriend."

She started to smile when I mentioned her boyfriend but checked herself. "See ya."

She kissed me on the cheek, hugged me, and left.

I called Kate several times a day for the next two weeks. Sometimes her roommate would say she was out. Sometimes there would be no answer. Sometimes, when there was an answer, the line would click off as soon as I spoke. I wouldn't see Kate again for years.

I didn't think it was possible for me to do worse than a 2.5, but I finished second semester with a 2.2. I was a bit distracted before finals, and the test files only work if you look at them.

I didn't go home that summer or any summer thereafter. I worked in Underwood's lab and waited tables at the restaurant. The first day of sophomore year, I got a letter from Dean Hightower asking me to set up an appointment with him to discuss my future in the pre-med program.

18

"You did O.K. your first semester, Walter. Not outstanding, but good enough. It's been downhill since then, wouldn't you agree?"

Dean Hightower sat behind his desk with my transcript on top of a manila file folder. My last semester's GPA was highlighted in yellow.

"Yes, sir."

"I have a responsibility to tell you that if your grades remain this low, it will be hard to recommend you for medical school. I also have a responsibility to the college to make sure those who we recommend are truly qualified."

"I've had a rough time lately," I said. "I can do better."

"Sometimes we make our own rough times," he said. "I'm sure you can do better, but you have to make sure what you're doing is what you want to be doing. Have you talked to your parents about your performance?

"No, sir."

"Perhaps you should. Nobody likes surprises, especially at 15 grand a year. Know what I mean?"

At the time I didn't know if I still thought I wanted to be a doctor. Sometimes I wonder if I ever really did. Most people in the pre-med program had a parent or grandparent in medicine; they had some idea what they were getting into. I'm sure some of those people were only doing it because it was what was expected of them, but most of them were willingly keeping up a family tradition. I was not the first in my family line to go to college, but I would be the first to graduate. There was no long-standing tradition in my family to follow, so I was doing what the rich kids I grew up around were doing. One guy from my high school was going to go to business school; he wanted to get an MBA so he could be a higher-powered executive than his father was. Kate's mother was an English teacher, and Kate wanted to go into publishing. My father was a salesman who bounced around from company to company. He didn't stay with one job long enough to have any company loyalty, and the things he sold were so disparate and uninteresting that it was hard for him to even feign excitement. I'm not ashamed or anything, it's just that his career was nothing to aspire to. He did well enough, I guess- his checks covering the half of my tuition I wasn't taking on debt for weren't bouncing.

"Mom?"

"Walter, is that you?" She answered the phone in her phone voice – it was her but she never sounded like herself when she talked on the phone.

"Can I talk to Dad?"

"Can you get the phone!?" she yelled, making no effort to distance her mouth from the receiver.

"Dad, I'm thinking about changing majors."

"What's that mean?"

"What I'm going to get my degree in. I'm thinking about switching out of the pre-med program."

"Does that mean you won't be becoming a doctor?"

"At least not a medical doctor."

I couldn't tell from his breathing if he was confused or disappointed. He didn't have the sleep apnea yet, but he had been putting on the pounds. His breathing sounded like horror-flick chase-scene breathing.

'I've been doing this research, and it's really interesting," I lied. "I'm thinking about changing majors and maybe getting my PhD"

"Will it take any longer?"

"It takes about the same amount of time. Instead of going to medical school, I'd go to graduate school."

"And when you're done, can your mom still say there's a doctor in the family?"

"I guess so."

"Well, if it doesn't take any longer and your mother can still tell her friends there's a doctor in the family, I guess it's okay. Do you want to tell Mom?"

"Can you fill her in," I said. I doubt he understood it enough to explain it to my mother, but I was pretty sure a PhD wouldn't cut it with my mom.

The next day I went back to Dean Hightower's office, and then to see Professor Underwood to get approval for my change in major. From there I went to Campus Pizza and ran into Francis, who was now the fraternity's social chairman.

"Anything going on this Saturday?"

"No," he said. "I think it's a slow weekend."

"I'd like to sponsor a continuous keg then. Twenty-five bucks enough?"

"That will cover the cheap stuff. What's the occasion?"

"I just quit pre-med."

"You dropping out?"

"No, just switching majors."

"I've done that a couple of times," he said. "Seven years of college…"

"…down the drain," I completed. Everyone in our fraternity (and probably everyone in every fraternity at the time) could finish any movie line from Stripes, Caddyshack and Animal House.

We clinked our Cokes to toast the genius of Harold Ramis, bowed our heads in memory of the departed John Belushi, and went back to our pizza.

19

By the middle of my senior year I had my name on six papers with Underwood. The first few times it was cool seeing my name in the scientific journals, but it was still hard to get too excited about what we were publishing. Our papers were mostly journal fodder. The drugs we were testing were already being tested on people. Everyone knew what the drugs did and how they did it, and if there were still any unknown surprises, the experiments we were doing weren't likely to turn up any of them up. We were trying new drug delivery methods, measuring physiologic responses, and checking on the potential for interactions with other drugs. We were just following recipes. The drug companies gave Underwood a list of questions, and we gave them the answers they were looking for. If Underwood kept them happy, they would go to Underwood when they had a new product to test. All the prestige was in new drug development; besides getting credit for the early work on a new product, getting in early assured there would be well-paying speaking engagements to promote the new drug if it got to market. Underwood also needed to maintain the industry-university partnerships. The idea that private endowments and government grants could fully fund academic institutions' research efforts was fading even before I got to college.

That what we published as our methods, and occasionally what we included in the results, was sometimes more science fiction than science didn't slow us down and was never questioned by journal editors or reviewers. Steve, in his last year and getting his PhD thesis together, and Martin insulated Underwood from the lab's raw data. If Underwood needed the results to look a certain way, then that is what he was shown by his graduate students. Underwood wasn't involved with the daily operation of the lab, and that allowed him to believe that the results coming out of his lab were completely legitimate. But he had to know corners were being cut.

I still felt like a guest in the lab, and I kept on just doing what I was told. Steve and Martin would tell me what to include in a paper and what to leave out, and that was how I would write it up. If they weren't exactly sure what a result should be, they would tell me to leave a blank, and they would fill in the numbers once they figured out what they needed. Eventually, I stopped thinking about whether the methods they were asking me to present resembled anything we did. One paper we submitted on the effect of a cholesterol medication on kidney function would only have shown accurate methods if it read, "Rats were given a medication for three weeks, killed, and then we threw them away."

Often we had to send our results to the sponsoring companies before we submitted them to the journals. The companies wanted to make sure their competitors didn't see anything that might help them develop a rival product, and they wanted to prevent the publication of potentially damaging data. Everyone working in the lab had to sign an agreement that we would not publish any data without permission of the company. Since we made sure the results matched what the companies were looking for, Underwood was almost always able to publish.

Midstate, like all universities, subscribed to the principle of publish or perish. Although the drug companies couldn't care less if data about a compound was published and would actively try to suppress unfavorable information, the university measured success by a simple count of the number of published papers. The last page of the graduate school's newsletter always had a bar graph indicating the number of publications each department had secured in the prior six months. A child psychology paper determining, "Why children prefer pudding to yogurt" had as much weight as the physics department's latest contribution to Super-String Theory. It's a ridiculous method of academic accounting, but it is what it is.

"We serve two masters," Underwood explained one afternoon after receiving a rare notice that data we collected (legitimate that time) on a new compound could not be included in our next series of publications.

"It's a balance. We have an interest and a duty to publish and share scientific information, but if the drug companies aren't able to set some ground rules, they will not be able to develop the drugs the public needs. Sometimes you have to suppress the data to advance the science."

We used other data from the same experiment to generate three papers, all of which were published. Each included some fabricated data or some indication that a procedure, which we had not done, was performed. The drug company got the data it needed to continue development of its compound, suppressed some that it didn't want to get out, and we got three more lines added to our CV's publication list

"Have you completed your interviews?" Underwood asked.

"I go to Penn next week. That's my last one."

"I hope you choose to stay here. Steve is finishing this year, and then is going to California to work for Celliscious. I don't know what kind of offers you're getting from the other programs, but make sure you bring your best one to me before signing."

I knew before I started graduate school interviews that I would probably end up staying at Midstate with Underwood. Besides being comfortable in the lab and knowing my way around the school, I knew Underwood was on the Board of several biotech and pharmaceutical companies, and that would pretty much guarantee a choice of jobs after getting my degree. It worked out well for Steve.

"Let me know when you get back from Penn."

"Thank you," I said. "I will."

20

"How've you been?" I said instead of "Hello" when Kate answered, hoping she wouldn't just hang up.

It was April. We'd be graduating in a month. I hadn't talked to Kate in almost three years, and if I had let college run out without trying, she would have moved on and I might never have found her again. This was before the Internet was big- you couldn't just Google somebody and find out everything about them from where they worked to when they last they used a public restroom. You can find pretty much anyone now, but I had a real chance of losing touch with her forever if I had let her move on then without trying to reach her.

"I've been good," she said. "Why are you calling?"

"I didn't want the last time I talked to you to be the last time I talked to you. I'm not calling for forgiveness," I lied. "But if it were available..."

"How could you have done that to me? I could have been in love with you."

That was the worst thing she could have said.

"I can't say anything to make it okay. I was wrong. I was an asshole. You know how it was. Except for you I never really had a girlfriend in high school. I got to college and..."

She cut me off, "You had a chance to get laid so you took it."

"It didn't mean anything to either of us. She had a boyfriend the whole time – I was a stand in. She came back last summer break with an engagement ring."

"Is that why you called? She's spoken for. Not getting any?"

I paused too long. I *had* slept with Lisa a few times after she got engaged, but that too had stopped. The whole relationship couldn't have meant all that much to either of us. After sleeping together nearly every week for two years, it was easy for both of us to drop it. We said "hi" when we passed each other, and there was nothing awkward about it. All break-ups should be like that.

"Uh…"

"What? You're still sleeping with her?"

"I…No."

"If you called to try and patch things up, you can forget it."

"I didn't. I did. Look, I didn't want to graduate without trying to talk to you again."

"Well you got that out of the way. Have fun in medical school."

"I'm not going to medical school. I'm staying here for grad school."

"Great. I took a job in New York."

"Who with?"

"It's not important. Bye, Walter."

"Well, if you ever want to talk…"

"I won't."

"If you do…"

"I won't"

"Either way, I'll be here."

"Don't wait for me."

"I'm *not* going to wait for you."

"What's that supposed to mean?"

"I'm not going to wait. But if you change your mind…"

"Bye."

She hung up.

I thought it went well.

21

During my second year of graduate school I saw how far I had come. Underwood brought a new undergrad up to the lab and asked Martin and me to show him around. The new kid looked around the lab while we finished recording some data. Like every new visitor to the lab, his first stop was at the Temple. Paulina the rat had since died, but in her running wheel we put a stuffed-animal rat wearing a tiny tiara. The *Sports Illustrated* calendar was on the same page that it was on the day I first entered the lab.

I asked Martin what we should tell the new guy about some of the scientific liberties we took with our procedures and our reports.

"We don't have to hide what we do here," Martin told me that morning. "It's how things are done. The important work is done completely – well mostly - legit, but you know there isn't the time or money or rats to do *all* the background work by the book. I was eased into that reality by Steve the same way we eased you into it when you first got here. We don't have to hide what we do, but you can't tell someone you just met that some of what comes out of this lab is nonsense. Once they see what we do and how we do it, they get it. Think about how you came around when you started."

"I know." I had. When I started the graduate program, I no longer had to ask Martin what to include or exclude in the project write-ups – I did it the way I knew it was to be done, the way Underwood would want it.

"So when the new kid gets here, just show him around. For the next couple months, he's just going to be feeding and weighing the animals anyway. We'll break him in when he's ready. You were easy; you picked it up right away. We'll have to see what this guy is like.

Some people just come here for a semester to get some research on their CVs, like the last guy."

I was easy.

Martin said that like it was nothing, but it hit me hard. *I was easy.* I don't remember one day being honest and the next, not. It was like those old Grecian Formula ads: *The change will be so gradual, even your friends won't notice.* But there I was, six years out from Bates's class and a natural at the art of fabrication.

My test would be the new guy. It was one thing to play along in someone else's game, but it was something else to explain the rules to another and have him buy it.

I was easy.

Maybe I was, but still.

I showed the new guy around, went over the procedures, and spent a half-hour telling him what a valuable experience my time in Underwood's lab had been and how it had changed my career choice.

"I was pre-med like you when I started at Midstate. After one semester in Underwood's lab, I knew this is what I had to do." I left out the part about having no real chance of getting into med-school. Details.

He ended up joining the lab. He stayed on for three years, but, unlike me, he did go on to medical school. He wasn't as fast a learner as I was, though. He didn't write up any of the papers during his first year, and even then he seemed surprised to learn that some things in the papers needed to be exaggerated for publication. But eventually he took this in and played along.

By the time I started work on my PhD thesis, the new guy could make up data with the best of them. I know this for a fact, because a lot of the data he made up found its way to my PhD thesis.

22

Dr. Underwood met me at the campus pub. The pub was half as large as it was when I started at Midstate. Just before I started at Midstate the drinking age had crept up from 18 (with pretty liberal attitudes as to what was accepted as valid ID) to 21 (with a computer scanner recording IDs and screening out even well-done fakes). Now, only seniors, grad students, and faculty could buy a beer on campus. One wing of the bar had been walled off to make more office space for the campus activity coordinators who coordinated the dry, and thus poorly attended, campus activities.

It was spring. The temperature was going up, and the amount of clothes people wore was going down. It was the same every year. The women you wanted to see the least of were the first to switch to the tight shorts and tank tops. I remember walking towards the campus activity building that housed the pub and turning my head this way, then that way, never quite believing what I was seeing.

I was a few minutes late, and Underwood had a table in the back of the pub. He was sipping what looked and smelled like scotch and was reading the graduate school newsletter.

"Sit down, Walter. I have the committee's report on your thesis."

The first go at my PhD thesis was made over winter break that year. A lot of candidates spent a whole year just writing the thing – I did mine the week between Christmas and New Year's. I gave it to Underwood, who took it with him to the shitter, reappeared 15 minutes later and said, "This reads like you wrote it over winter break. I expected somewhat more, Mr. Most. Please redo."

I turned it in for the second time two months after that, and my presentation was in April. The committee had since met, and

Underwood had the official response letter in a manila folder under his copy of the campus newsletter.

"The committee spent a long time discussing your thesis, Walter."

I couldn't read the guy. No smile, no disappointed look. Nothing. If he played poker, and I'm sure he did not, he would clean up. My heart was pounding in my neck; I started to sweat. I was trying to think ahead as to what I'd say and do if my thesis was rejected. The crap I handed in the first time *was* crap, but I thought I had turned it into something decent. I even asked one of the English majors to make sure the commas were in the right places. If this wasn't good enough, I wasn't sure I'd be able to put together something that was.

"Can I buy you a drink?" he said. "Beer? Scotch?"

"If it's good news, I'll take a beer. If it's bad, a shot of whiskey."

"Bud or Sam Adams?"

"Hypothetically?"

"No. Your thesis was accepted, and you are being recommended for your doctorate. Congratulations."

I got my beer, Underwood ordered another scotch, and then he got to business.

"Have you thought about where you are going to go from here."

"I started looking at some jobs. I've had some phone conversations, but I haven't set up any interviews yet."

"I could certainly put in a good word for you at some colleges. I know a few department chairmen that are looking for junior research faculty with your background. Have you considered industry?"

I had thought about working R&D for a biotech or pharmaceutical company. The starting money was considerably less than what was being paid by the bigger academic centers, but advancement was much slower in the university setting. You started out as an assistant professor, had to work your ass off under a mentor, and got very little reward or recognition for about seven years. Then you were eligible for promotion to associate professor. The money was a little better, but after seven more years, it was up or out; either you got yourself funded and promoted to full professor, or it was teaching introductory science at a community college. Life turned nice when you became a full professor – good money, good perks – but you definitely paid your dues for a long time.

Working for the biotechs had its own risks. A lot of companies failed when the products they were developing just didn't work. Fortunes had been made, however, by people who started working on compounds that had initials instead of names. If you received stock options instead of a salary, you could find yourself a millionaire if the products did well. I know this to be true, because for a few weeks I had Biotechna options worth over five million dollars, and I think if I could have cashed them in I would have retired and avoided the mess I'm in now.

"I would be willing to look at anything," I told him.

He turned over my thesis notification letter and wrote on the back.

"I'm giving you the name and number of a fellow I know at Biotechna. He's head of R&D, which sounds prestigious, except there are only three employees in the R&D Department. I'm an advisor to their board. I think you might fit in."

"Thanks, I'll call."

"An academic career isn't what it used to be," Underwood said, taking a sip of his scotch. "It has worked out well for me, but if I was starting out today, I would go a different path. Too much red tape. Too many demands. Institutions are so caught up in the money they don't care about the science. We have to sing louder and louder for our supper each year. One more bad year in the stock market and the research endowment might dry up altogether. Enough about that. If you decide to go academic, I'll support you. But give my friend a call either way."

"I will."

He put the paper back in the envelope with my thesis acceptance letter, slid it across the table, and held up his scotch.

"Congratulations and a toast: to Dr. Most."

We clinked glasses. My family could be proud: a doctor in the family.

PART 4

Biotechna

23

The back hallway of Biotechna was lined with motivational posters touting the benefits of 'Perseverance' and 'Leadership.' The 'Teamwork' one showed a football lineman making an obviously painful block so that a running back could spin into the end zone. The lineman's head was at an impossible angle, and his feet were off the ground. The caption read: There is no *I* in team.

I was sitting outside Art Michelson's office, waiting for my interview to begin. I had about ten minutes with nothing to do but stare at the posters and consider the possibilities. There is no *I* in team. But you could get *me*, so there was a *me* in team. You could get *eat meat* if you reused some of the letters. The ads in the back of the airline magazines suggest those posters boost corporate morale. Does anyone think those posters motivate the unmotivated? Those posters are about as honest as that electronic voice that tells you over and over again, 'Your call is extremely important to us,' while you wait for a customer service representative. Who would want to work for a company that needed motivational posters to motivate? Who would want to employ someone that responded to a motivational poster? I was thinking about leaving when Michelson's door opened.

"Dr. Most. Sorry to have kept you waiting."

Art Michelson, the head of R&D at Biotechna, shook my hand as I stood up. In Michelson's white button-down shirt I could see the afterimage of the poster I was staring at when he opened his door: a track runner with finish-line tape stretched across his chest. The text on the poster was green, so 'Success' appeared in a red above his belt line.

"Great art," I said, sweeping my hand down the hall indicating the ridiculous motivational posters. I was too slow remembering that his name was Art, and greeting him as "Great Art" might not have been the way to go.

Michelson looked down the hall, stopping at each poster like his head was connected to his body by some kind of ratcheting system. "Really? I think they came with the building, they were hanging there when we moved in."

"I've always thought the whole idea of those motivational posters was kind of silly," I said.

"Why'd you say 'great art,' then?" He seemed dissatisfied.

"Uh…In case…" It didn't take me long to fuck this one up, I thought.

"I was being humble," Art said. "Like poster Number 3 down there suggests." He pointed at the *humble* poster, and then his chest. "I picked these out. I framed them. I hung them. I take their messages very personally, and I believe they represent the essential elements of our corporate culture."

I figured the interview was about to be over. I didn't know if Underwood would be willing to help me again after Biotechna dismissed me in less than five minutes.

Michelson clapped me on the back. "Just fucking with you. Relax. Don't bullshit me – I do love playing the head games, though. Almost as much as I love thinking about the money we're all going to make when CXR gets approved. Sorry, Walter. I don't know where these posters come from, and if I had ten extra minutes the same time I had a screwdriver, I'd replace them. But what do I care? They do their job and I do mine. Come in."

I was in Michelson's office for two hours before he offered me a job. He spent the first half-hour catching me up on the history of CXR. Michelson had been a biochemist at Aetearnal Pharmaceutical Company when he accidentally discovered CXR while working on a compound they called VV. Aetearnal was the name assumed when two more reasonably named pharmaceutical companies merged – this was at a time when corporations thought their images would be best served by giving themselves names that sounded like words but weren't, most of which seemed to start with the letter A.

While performing one of the chemical separations for VV, Michelson found a compound that had yet to be cataloged in VV production process. He separated it out on the sly and gave it the name CXR. He started keeping separate notes. When he had enough of the CXR purified, he gave some to the animal guys at Aetearnal who unknowingly included the CXR with the VV in their research. The first step in the development of a lot of these compounds is to isolate them, then give them to animals and see what happens. If you measure enough parameters, you might find something you like, and if what you find represents something that could be useful down the road in people, you start a research line. There's less than a one in a thousand chance of hitting on something big, but if you do, it could be a billion-dollar product. The odds are against any given company, but if you think about those suckers that line up to play the lottery every week, a one-in-a-thousand chance on biotech research doesn't seem like such a silly gamble any more. Michelson looked at the initial results from the CXR animals and thought he might have something.

So Michelson took his notes on CXR to Fred Mathews, who raised the venture capital to start the company. The day Mathews had the cash together and secured the building, Michelson cleared out his desk and began the development of CXR at the new company, Biotechna. Aetearnal never had any idea that Michelson essentially stole a compound that by Michelson's contract they had the rights to.

That was five years before I arrived, and CXR was now in Phase II human trials – if these were successful, they would start the big Phase III trials that would determine if CXR would be approved by the FDA. Although the human trials seemed to be going well, Michelson was thinking ahead to the final application to the FDA, and he knew they would need to include more animal safety data as part of their presentation. That's where I came in. A lot of the initial work was done at Aetearnal and was thought to represent the VV compound at the time. Michelson knew the results really represented CXR, but some of the initial work had to be repeated at Biotechna. Michelson had been overseeing the animal work himself, but now he worried it would look suspicious if he went back to the animal safety work. They wanted to hire me to do the small animal work to fill in the holes for the FDA application.

After his presentation he showed me the lab. There were no locked doors or security checks – the compound's security was the 24-hour guards stationed at the entrance to the technology complex and the closed circuit monitors that the guards watched when they weren't checking IDs.

He showed me the lab where I would be working. There were a few hundred small animal cages along the back wall, all empty.

"I think you will find our facilities a little nicer than those encountered at the university," He said.

I did.

After the tour we sat in his office. He sat with his elbows on his desk, his hands forming a steeple below his chin.

"Now, for your compensation package," he folded his fingers down as if the next thing he would do would be open the door and show me the people.

"The cash portion of your pay can only be $40,000. Full benefits, of course."

"Cash portion?" I said.

"You will also be granted options on Biotechna stock. Ten thousand shares for signing, and an additional ten thousand shares as you complete each of these milestones." He pointed to the research plan on the spreadsheet in front of him.

Biotechna stock was trading at $1.32 when we met. I had looked at the stock-chart before my interview. It had been higher, but the initial Phase II results were mixed, and the stock plummeted to around 50 cents. They had recently obtained some more encouraging results and the stock nearly tripled to its current levels. There was another company, similar to Biotechna, which, after some good results, watched its stock run up from \$3 to \$100. There was no reason something like that couldn't happen at Biotechna. Between my signing bonus and the milestones, I would have 50,000 in essentially free shares of the company's stock. If CXR was successful, that could turn into a lot of money.

I took the job.

24

Dr. Fred Mathews started Biotechna on his thirtieth birthday, and he was still one of the youngest CEOs in the industry. He wasn't a whiz kid; he wasn't one of those precocious teens who drop out of college because school is slowing them down, develop some idea in a garage and becomes the industry leader. He was just a rich kid who stayed in school long enough to get his PhD because he had nothing better to do and didn't want to have to go to work. When his trust fund kicked in at 18, he was guaranteed an annual income of $200,000 per year for the rest of his life, more during good stock market years. His college performance was notable only for his achieving a 2.0 grade average by scoring a "C" in every course he took for four years straight. He was sure it must have been some kind of school record, but there was no formal acknowledgment of his achievement.

He insisted on being called Dr. Fred, enjoying the sound of the formal "doctor" juxtaposed with the somewhat goofy sounding "Fred." When he was interviewed on one of the business channels, it took most of the 30 seconds allotted to the earnings report of his small biotech company to get through the establishment of the proper appellation.

"Good Morning, Dr. Mathews," the talking head interviewer would begin.

"Dude, Dr. Mathews is my father. Call me Fred."

"Okay, Fred, can you tell the viewers your company's progress with…"

"That's Dr. Fred."

The exchange was generally followed by an uncomfortable pause, and a commercial break would be called for by the reporter who had lost his train of thought. Over time Dr. Mathews, Dr. Fred to you, was asked to give fewer and fewer interviews.

When he did give an interview, Mathews came across like the stoner he was. He had, like many children of privilege, easy access to drugs growing up, and apparently, he had tried them all. He bragged at a company party how, while in high school, he was arrested for felony possession of marijuana with intent to distribute. He was pulled over for driving erratically, and the cop asked to see what was in his trunk.

"Dude, you had to see it," Mathews said. "I had the bags of pot packed in so tight, when the cop asked me to open the trunk, they popped out all over the highway. Man, it was awesome." Mathew's net worth exceeded twenty million dollars.

"I got it down to misdemeanor possession and just had to do some community service. I convinced the DA the pot was for personal consumption – which it was. I can afford to share, I never sold an ounce in my life."

Even when he was talking science, it came out like he was talking surfing.

"Like, these antibodies are like, 'I need some antigens, baby' and when they find them they're like, 'tasty.'" He'd lace his fingers together to demonstrate the bonding of antigen and antibody.

And, although he sounded like a doofus most of the time, he was like most of the rich-kid stoners I grew up around: brilliant.

So long as Dr. Fred Senior could tell his associates that Fred was doing something productive with his life, Fred had free run. He stayed in school for as long as possible, which suited Fred senior just fine. He insisted he only used drugs recreationally, but with his family's money and low targets for academic performance, Fred had a lot of time for recreation.

Fred Mathews met Art Michelson while Fred was still in graduate school. Michelson had the unwanted duty of road-show point man for Aetearnal Pharmaceutical. Every year, at the end of winter, universities invited industry representatives to job fairs – colleges wanted to maximize their job placement statistics so they could justify tuition levels to incoming freshman; companies wanted their pick of the new graduates so they could have first shot of the best and brightest. Those fresh out of school were usually the hardest working and the least likely to object to unfavorable terms in a contract.

Michelson had done the college shows three years in a row and was getting sick of them. Three weeks of driving college to college, setting up and breaking down a display board every day, dozens of paper cuts from all the resumes. With each school he was less able to fake the excitement that a good job-fair presentation required – his lack of enthusiasm was easy for the students to read.

Michelson first met Mathews at one of the road show presentations, and, as Michelson told me during my interview, he's glad there weren't any sharp objects near while Michelson was talking to him or he might have stabbed Mathews or slashed his own wrists to make it stop.

"The guy wouldn't leave," Michelson told me. "Six hours of "dude" and "hey, man." He talked about everything except biotechnology. The only break I got from him was when he went to get lunch, and I'm pretty sure he came back stoned, or at least more stoned than he was before lunch. His was the only resume I collected that day, and the company measured road-show success by weighing the collected resumes."

That was Michelson's last year on the road. He had already started his work on CXR. He knew he was going to make a break for it, but didn't have any specific plans. His supervisors were impressed with the long hours he was putting in, unaware that the overtime was for a personal project, not the company's benefit.

Michelson's epiphany came while he was drinking a beer in bed, surfing channels looking for Baywatch or something like it. Mathews Sr. had died, and CNN reported that the Fred Mathews Foundation had made a 3-million-dollar donation to the some philharmonic orchestra. The senior Fred Mathew, as the news report related, had

138

patented a piece of plastic that was essential in the process that allowed rapid genetic sequencing, and he had been receiving royalties on every decoded base pair since.

The TV then cut to the Fred Mathews whom Michelson had met a few months prior.

"My Dad was like, a righteous dude, man. The two things he loved the most were classical music and DNA."

When asked what the younger Fred was going to do with himself, he said he was in no hurry to start a career but "I know it will be something in science. I'm finishing up my PhD, and our family has enough money, like, to do some good, you know. That's what Dad would have wanted." He then looked to the sky, raised a fist over his head, closed his eyes and said, "Rock on, Pops."

CNN cut to the finals of a dog show.

The next day Michelson dug up Mathews's resume, took home all his notes for CXR, and made a dozen phone calls trying to set up a meeting with Mathews. By the end of the week, Mathews was president and CEO of Biotechna, Michelson was head of R&D and senior vice president. After Michelson resigned from Aetearnal, security watched him the entire time he was packing his desk to make sure he didn't take any proprietary information with him. It was too late.

After my interview with Michelson, he took me to meet Mathews.

"Michelson says you're our guy," Mathews said.

He was spread out on a leather sofa in his office. In one corner of his office was a tall Yamaha rack system with some expensive headphones on top. His desk was cluttered with paper, and incense burners were being used as paperweights. Although the office was air-conditioned, there was a large window fan pointing out the window. There was a towel hung on the inside doorknob, undoubtedly for keeping the smoke from entering the hallway. Except for the bong, the fan, the towel, and the incense, it looked like what I would have expected any biotech start-up CEO's office to look like.

"Nice to meet you, Dr. Mathews."

"Call me Fred."

"Okay, Fred."

"Dude, it's Dr. Fred."

That was the only time I recall Mathews looking completely serious in the two years I knew him.

"Michelson tells me we have some animal stuff we have to get through, and you're going to be the one to do it."

"That's what we talked about. I worked with similar models in Underwood's lab."

'Whose?"

Underwood was on the board of Biotechna, but it took a few moments for it to register with Mathews.

"Oh. Right. Underwood," Mathews nodded. "Smart man. Knew my father. When can you start?"

"Monday?"

"Cool. Monday. Party on."

25

"Are you sure these protocols are right?" I asked Michelson.

"Some of the earlier CXR was probably still contaminated with the VV. Keep adjusting the dosage until you find the one that gives the effect we are looking for without any of the liver toxicity."

"All right," I told him, "but it's been a few months and nothing is looking too promising. You sure this stuff works?"

"It's all work that has been done before. The Phase II data in people has been pretty good for the enzyme markers we're using – we won't know until the Phase IIIs if it really helps people, but it will. Besides playing with the dosages, why don't you triple the number of rats you're using- maybe that will get you the P values we need."

It took me about six months and more than 2,000 rats to find a dose that showed the enzyme readings we needed without killing the rats. Then I had to write up the data as though the dosage was the one we expected to use all along. The increased number of rats made it easier to find a difference that ordinarily would have been considered inconsequential. That's a game everyone plays. If you flip a coin ten times and get six heads, you wouldn't be suspicious that the coin is weighted. If you flipped it 10,000 times and got 6,000 heads, you should suspect a cheat. The statistical analysis done in research works the same way. If one drug cures six people in a group of ten and another drug cures four people in another group of ten, it wouldn't be convincing that one drug is better than the other. If in groups of 10,000 one drug cured 6,000 and another cured 4,000, you would request the 6,000-curing drug if you were so afflicted.

The system can be gamed. If you know the difference between drugs is tiny, but you need to demonstrate *some* difference, you do the experiment with lots of subjects so you find results that are statistically significant. If you are a competitor, you might do an experiment with few subjects to show there is no important difference. We were trying to show CXR worked, and the easy adjustment to the work I was doing was to increase the number of rats I tested. It worked.

Experiments whose results were not what we were looking for were discarded, the data filed away and never fully analyzed. When results pointed our way, those protocols became the ones we completed and reported. If it were just about the science, we would have saved and presented every piece of information we obtained. We weren't really looking for the information, however. We were assembling a sales pitch to bring to the FDA to get approval of a drug that could make us all a lot of money.

In the snake oil days, salesmen could offer treatment-success testimonials to prospective buyers to promote their wares. Over the past hundred years, a system has evolved, wherein products need to get approved by the FDA and be endorsed by medical societies before there is any chance of selling them. To get over those hurdles requires the presentation of information that sounds scientific. A lot of research is just lipstick on pigs- crappy data dressed up as high-quality research. What I was working on was just a minor part of what would be assembled into a package for a government agency. It didn't have to be pretty, it didn't have to be complete; It just had to be there. We could include any of it we wanted and leave out what appeared unfavorable.

"If the FDA wants to look at our work more closely," Michelson said, "it's not like they are going to come here and look at the rats. They're just going to want to see more of the data."

He was hinting that inconclusive results might need to be adjusted. The rats would be long gone by the time the FDA requested more information – they would just want to see the data sheets. When the rats were dead and gone, who could say an enzyme level was higher or lower than what we said it was? It was the human trials that would determine if the drug got approved or not, anyway. My work was just a formality.

Each of my experiments took about a week to complete, but it took weeks of sampling and processing the rats' frozen livers and kidneys to get the measurements of this obscure enzyme that would be different between the two groups of rats. After a year and a half, I thought I had all the results we needed. It wasn't pretty, but it looked scientific.

"Nice job on the enzyme data," Mathews and Michelson told me after they reviewed my final reports.

"Thanks," I said. "I don't know how useful it will be for the application."

"Are you kidding me? Mathews says it's gold. We're starting to get the Phase III data from the human trials now, and we have two guys working on the application package. There's a bookmark where your animal work fits in, and this stuff is perfect." He slapped his palm with my rolled up data as he spoke.

"If you say so."

"Get ready to get rich, Dr. Most. When word gets out that we sent the application to the FDA, the stock is going to the moon." Now he used my rolled-up data as a pointer.

"I don't mean to piss on the parade," I said. "But do you really think the data so far has been compelling?"

"The FDA just has to buy that CXR is safe and effective – and I think we'll show that," Michelson said. "I would have hoped the effect was greater, but a lot of drugs have been approved that do a lot less. The investment people don't care about the science, they just want to hear about the sales potential. So long as the application is complete, they'll invest."

"You think CXR will get approved?"

"We have enough subgroup comparisons in the final experiments to make it look like it has some benefit. There haven't been any safety concerns. Maybe effective plus not dangerous equals money in the bank."

For the next few weeks I did nothing but work on my section of the FDA application. It was more fact than fiction, but there were plenty of questions for which the answers just didn't exist. The forms were ridiculous and, I was told, had to be filled out exactly like the FDA wanted or the entire application would come right back. The FDA keeps the process Byzantine under the philosophy that if you couldn't fill out a complicated form, how could you perform complicated science? One has nothing to do with the other, but it makes some twisted sense.

26

The champagne corks were popped open as soon as the FedEx guy pulled out of the parking lot with the FDA application.

Mathews stood on a chair and raised his glass. "Dudes, I know all that just happened is like the mailman came, but that was awesome. To CXR."

There were twenty of us in the hall outside of Mathews' office: two sales guys, three from the new marketing department, the lab techs and the secretaries.

"Why don't we take this party down to the conference room," Mathews said. "Walter, Art, come in my office. We'll join the others in a minute."

Art and I sat in his office as he turned on his window fan and stuffed a towel under his door. He took a copy of the Physicians Desk Reference off of his bookshelf. I thought he was going to show us where he thought CXR would be included, but when he opened the book I saw that it had been hallowed out to make room for baggies filled with pot, cocaine, and who knew what else. It was his stash.

Mathews rolled a joint as he talked. "Gentlemen, congratulations." He took a deep inhale and passed it to Michelson who followed suit and passed it to me. I took a hit and handed it back to Mathews.

"I've just got off the phone with Dewey financial. They are interested in investing in CXR, and they told me they want us to make a presentation after our application is in. I've been bank-rolling this operation so far, but if we are going to go into production, we are going to need some serious investment money. We're meeting them the day after tomorrow."

"Where's Dewey?" Michelson asked.

"Manhattan. I'm going down tomorrow, and you're going with me."

I still thought about Kate all the time, but it was always just brief flashes. I'd see someone with hair like hers and imagine it could be her, or someone would say the name Kate and I'd turn, expecting her to be there. Just flashes: Her smile, she and I walking somewhere, Kate in Bates's class, our first time together. Maybe it was the pot kicking in, but when Mathews said Manhattan, where I believed Kate was working, I felt I needed to go with them.

"Can I go too?"

"Sorry, dude. I'm doing the money presentation, and Art's presenting the science. Three's a crowd. No worries."

This time it was the pot – I started laughing when he said three's a crowd. Then all three of us started laughing, and the joint made a few more rounds.

"Let's join the others," Mathews said. "They got food in the conference room."

It was just Art, Fred and I after the rest of the staff had gone home. Back in Fred's office Mathews and Michelson did lines of coke while I hung on to a joint. It got blurry after that. Fred kept taking baggies out of the PDR and instructing us on the most efficient ways to ingest what he was offering. There were no syringes, so I didn't think we could get into too much trouble.

Mathews was shaking me awake the next morning- I had passed out in his office.

"You seen Art?"

"No."

"His car is still here, let's find him."

Art was passed out in the men's room, propped up against a toilet. When I turned his head, the flush lever had left a deep red imprint in his forehead. He opened one eye and turned towards the bowl to vomit.

Mathews said, "Looks like the PhD can't handle his PCP. Let's go, Art. We have to leave for NYC. in two hours."

Michelson let out an incomprehensible moan and then either farted or shit his pants. He waved us away.

"I don't think he's going to make it, Walter. I guess it's you. Can you be ready to leave by 11?"

27

I was able to get home, clean up, and be ready for Mathews' limo and the ride to New York. That evening we met our contacts from Dewey Financial Corp. at Morton's Steak House– there's one in most big cities. They try to make it seem like a local joint, but in six-point type at the bottom of the menu is a list of 50 or so other locations– I had been to the one in Boston. There, the sports page clippings hanging over the urinals cover the Red Sox instead of the Yankees, but otherwise it's the same. The meal starts with this guy – not the waiter, the pre-waiter – who comes to your table with this rolling butcher block and shows you the meat selections for the evening. Three-inch thick tenderloins, giant rib-eyes, potatoes the size of melons, all on display to get you pumped up for what you are about to receive. It's the lobster I feel bad for. It was the same set-up in New York as it was in Boston. If you get there early, when the meat wagon comes around there's this playful lobster running around the butcher block – it's like a three pounder. The lobster crawls over the other entrees, almost falls off the block, and playfully feels the pre-waiter's face with its antennae when lifted up for all at the table to inspect. (Tourists have been known to ask the pre-waiter to take their pictures with the lobster.) By the end of the night, the same tired lobster is still doing the rounds. Maybe they can't serve it once it's been on tour, and at $23 a pound, they're only going to sacrifice one of those babies a night. By 10PM the lobster is barely moving, no longer exploring with its antennae, and goes limp when picked up. The show then becomes a crustacean *Weekend at Bernie's*. The original pre-waiter has finished his shift and been replaced, but the one lobster is on all night. I imagine they don't sell as many at the end of the evening.

We were seated at seven o'clock, so the lobster still had some life in it. I ordered the rib-eye. Mathews ordered the lobster, and the two from Dewey had the tenderloin.

The Dewey men were both wearing dark suits with white shirts. Peter Markow, the younger of the two and probably not yet forty, was wearing a bow tie. The older man was graying but not a white out yet. He wore a dark satin tie and carried himself like he thought he should be in charge, but he wasn't. They seemed to know all about Fred Mathews, but asked typical questions. They asked Mathews if he had been to the city before (yes), what he missed most about the West Coast (tasty waves for surfing), and made other small talk designed to fill the air between dinner and business.

The older of the two bankers, Roger Winthrop, excused himself after the appetizer.

"Hey Pete," Fred Mathews asked. "What time is our presentation tomorrow?"

"One o'clock. Will that be all right?"

"That's excellent. I was thinking about a little after-dinner party. Get to know each other a little better before we hit you up for the ten mil. Know what I mean?"

"I don't know what Roger has planned…"

"No dude, just me and you. Just us upper ranks. Know what I mean?"

Fred gestured at his nose, and if you weren't looking for anything, you would have missed it, and if you had seen it, it might not have meant anything to you, but no doubt Mathews was offering to share some cocaine after dinner.

Winthrop returned from the bathroom, and conversation picked up where it had left off. There was no further discussion of our business meeting that would take place the next day or of Fred's offer of an after dinner meeting between him and Pete.

The next day's meeting wasn't until one, so I had a few hours to kill in the morning. I looked up Kate and thought I'd give her a call.

I'm lying a bit. Even though I was hung over after the office party at Biotechna, when I found out I would be going to New York, I hit the internet and spent an hour getting a reasonably certain work address and phone number for Kate. There were several hits for "Kate Mason" and "New York," But only one that looked like it was at a publishing house.

Her firm was located midtown, off Fifth Avenue, and occupied three floors of a nondescript, tan brick building. Just inside the revolving door was a bank of elevators and a sign indicating where each occupant could be found. I got off at the lowest of the publisher's floors and headed towards the receptionist.

"Can I see Kate Mason?"

The secretary looked up when I got off the elevator and, even though she saw me coming towards her, she looked back down at the magazine she was reading. She was chewing gum and wearing those telephone headphones they always show on the heads of the operators that are standing by. She didn't look like she would be making much effort to be helpful. I was close enough to see she was reading *People*, but she still didn't look up.

"Excuse me," I said.

"Can I help you," still not looking up.

"I was wondering if I could see Miss Mason?"

"Do you have an appointment?"

"No."

"She's not in this morning"

"Why did you ask if I had an appointment if she's not in anyway?"

"Are you serious?"

"Yes."

She rolled her eyes. "Let me call up and see. Maybe she's back and didn't check in."

"Miss Mason…Yes…There's someone here for you…A…What was your name again?"

"Walter. Walter Most. She should know who I am."

"A Mr. Most. Yes, Walter. I don't know. I don't know. He didn't say. I will. I will."

"She's back in, but she is very busy this morning."

"Can I see her?"

"You can go up – Floor 26 – but she has another appointment in 15 minutes, so you will need to be quick."

"Thanks. Did she tell you to ring her in 15 minutes in case I'm not out of there?"

"Hey, You're smarter than you look."

"Thanks."

The elevator opened up to a Floor 26 full of cubicles – it was like what you'd expect Dilbert's office to look like. The corner offices were large with glass doors and one panel of glass next to the door. You could see into those offices when you stood at the door, but from anywhere else in the cubicle pit, the contents and occupants of the office were out of sight. These larger offices were for the executive editors. Kate didn't have one of these, but she wasn't a cubicle dweller either. She had one of the smaller offices that lined the perimeter. Better than a cubicle, but not quite a corner.

Three cubicle dwellers (junior editorial assistants) directed me to Associate Editor Kate Mason's office. It was small; if I were to lay across the floor in either direction with my feet against one wall, my hands could reach the opposite. At least she had a door – and one you could close and not be seen inside. I imagined that the associate editors did most of the real work, and thus needed all the real privacy. The grunt work in the pit probably didn't require too much concentration, and the higher-ups in the corner offices only needed to make sure everything turned out all right.

A quick scan of Kate's office revealed no boyfriend pictures – a good sign as it had been a few years since I had talked to her. I knew she wasn't saving herself for me.

"What are you doing here?" she asked.

I didn't expect much more of a greeting. The last time she saw me I had that post-coital glow, and it wasn't Kate I had coitaled with.

"I'm down in the city for the day, and I was wondering if you wanted to grab dinner. I have a meeting for work at one, but I'm free after that."

"You've got to be kidding me."

"I'm not."

"There is no way."

"Why not? It's just dinner."

"Anyway, Walter, I'm seeing someone."

"Is it serious?"

"Are you serious?"

"Your secretary asked me that. Yes, I'm serious."

"Walter, I mean it. I'm seeing someone, and I don't think …even if I wanted to …and right now I don't think I do."

"Well, there's some hope if you're stuttering. Come on. Have dinner with me. I'm only here for today."

"Walter."

"Kate, I'm sorry. I know I shouldn't have just come up, but there isn't a day I don't think about you. I know how stupid I was. I know what an asshole I was. I'd do it differently if I could do it over."

"You sound like you've gotten a little smarter."

"Come on, who is this guy – I don't see any pictures. Is he what, deformed?" I did a hunchback impression. A laugh slipped out, but she checked herself.

"Very funny. No, he's very good looking. I don't have any pictures because…" she paused and looked towards her door.

"He works here, doesn't he?" That secretary would have been proud of my figuring that out. I probably should have pumped the secretary for some information before coming up; she *was* reading *People* and must have had some interest in gossip. Kate kept her gaze at the door.

"Sort of."

"Is it your boss?"

Nothing. She looked down at her desk.

"What, is he married?"

She looked up at me. Her eyes said he was.

"Kids?"

"She wants them, he doesn't"

"Kate, come on. You're better than that. Even if you want nothing to do with me, you deserve better than that. Come out with me tonight. Your married boss can't mind. We'll just catch up – no strings, no nothing."

"Walter, I can't."

"Okay," I said, backing towards the door. "I've got to go prepare for my meeting."

"Where are you staying?"

Bingo.

"Marriott Marquis. Will you come by?"

"No. If I change my mind, maybe I'll call."

Her phone rang, she hit speaker.

"Miss Mason," her secretary's voice said, "your next appointment is here."

"Thanks, Heather, send him up."

"Heather told me your next appointment was with a woman."

"Did she?" She looked down at her planner. "So it is. Either way."

"No. Wait. She did say it was a woman."

"Walter!"

I left. I was hoping she would get up for a kiss or hug or handshake or anything, but she just said goodbye, held my gaze for an extra second, then looked down at the papers on her desk.

I still had some time before the meeting at Dewey's, so I went back to the hotel and waited for Kate to call. She didn't.

28

So Roger Winthrop, the older of the two Dewey men, and I sat in the silence-strained conference room waiting for Pete Markow and Fred Mathews. When I arrived, the secretary offered me a choice of coffee, tea or soda. After 45 minutes of waiting, she offered again and provided refills. A few people had poked into the conference room, checking on the meeting's progress. Ten million dollars would be huge for Biotechna, but it was only a medium-sized deal for Dewey. Still, Mathews was the head of our company, and only Markow had authority to make the final decision for Dewey, and both were well past being just a little late.

"Why don't you get started? We can tape the presentation for Pete in case he has questions or needs to catch up later. He's gone through the preliminary information and knows most of what you're going to talk about."

One of Pete's assistant vice presidents wanted to get things moving. Fred and Pete had gone out after our dinner, but it was now past two in the afternoon. Where the hell were they?

I asked for a moment to prepare before starting. Instead of preparing, I went outside to call the hotel to check for any messages from Kate. There were none.

"I guess I'll get started," I said when I returned. There was no sign of the bosses.

I gave a decent overview of CXR and of the company. I wasn't prepared for any of the financials, and I didn't understand the more technical details of the potential financial arrangement with Dewey, so I didn't try to bullshit them. I knew the biologic stuff cold, but was weak on the organic chemistry that went into CXR's development and manufacturing. I practiced what would be my part of the presentation before we left, so I had most of it down. Roger Winthrop asked a few questions about CXR's production process- not an area I knew much about. I learned in graduate school that when people ask questions about something that you wouldn't think they knew much about, most of the time they didn't know anything about what they are asking, but were trying to make themselves look as though they did. It's a subtle, but advanced form of bullshitting. I didn't really know much about the production process, but I gambled that Roger and everyone else at the meeting didn't either – at dinner Roger said he majored in finance, had worked at Dewey since graduating college, and never once indicated that he had any training or interest in anything related to organic chemistry manufacturing processes. So, I faked my way through the answer, spouting some catch lines about an in-line technique that I remembered from the one-page glossy we used for a press release.

I was halfway through the PowerPoint presentation, zapping slides' bullet points with a laser pointer, when Fred and Pete entered the conference room.

Except for the sunglasses, Fred looked about right. Pete looked like he was up all night partying. About right, because he was. He had bags under his bloodshot eyes, his nose glistened with nasal discharge, and he had not shaved. His tie, the same one from the night before, was crooked and his top button was undone. He sat down at the conference table, belched under his breath a few times, then rested his face in his hands. Fred sat next to me.

"Cool, you're almost done," Fred said to himself, giving me a thumbs up.

"Can someone get me some coffee?" Pete said. Two of Pete's assistants stood and one left for coffee.

"I'd like to thank Walter for the awesome job kicking things off here," Fred said, standing. "I see we're up to the financials. Let me tell you our ideas..."

Fred spoke like one of those talking head MBAs you see on the business channel. He had switched off the surfer dude and sounded like someone who knew what he was saying. Pete looked like he was going to ask one of us if we could cut off his head.

Fred presented his financing proposal in five minutes, passed around sheets outlining the deal, and asked for questions. Pete asked for some Motrin and said nothing else. The others were dumbstruck. This was my first and only ten million dollar presentation, and I suspect it was not typical. We thanked them and left together.

"What happened last night?" I asked Fred as we stepped out on the sidewalk.

Fred had taken off his sunglasses in the elevator to reveal eyes as red as Pete's had been. He put his sunglasses back on when we got outside.

Fred said, "That guy can't hold his 'shrooms."

"What happened last night?"

"I wrapped up the deal is what happened."

"What happened?"

"Just an after-hours party. We went back to my room for some Tequila shots and blow. The hookers and mushrooms were an afterthought, but I must say, they worked out quite well."

"You wrapped up a 10-million-dollar deal over blow, hookers and mushrooms?"

"Hey, the deal was going to happen – I just lubed it."

"What happened?"

"Less than you think, man. Pete said he didn't get high that often, but he could be into some coke. Let me tell you, a couple toots and he becomes mister paranoid – going off about how his wife was going to kill him, the cops are going to bust in on us – anything he could think of. I had a phone number from the last time I was in NYC, and I called to have some girls sent over. When they arrived, he got more agitated. I told him some 'shrooms might mellow him out. For about an hour after his first nibble, he alternated between barfing and explosive diarrhea, then passed out in my bathtub with his pants around his ankles. When he woke up this morning with his pants off, he figured something must have happened with the women, and he begged me not to tell his wife. I suggested once we get the deal done, you and I would leave town, and no one would be the wiser about our little party. We signed the papers in his office before coming to the presentation."

"So the presentation was for nothing?"

"It had to be done, dude. But it turned out to be just a formality."

"What happened with the hookers?"

"We all lost interest when Pete started puking. I paid them and sent them on their way. Once the papers on our financing are final, I'll let Pete know that nothing happened with the girls. I'll let him freak for a few days, though. You can't trust those financial types, you know."

"So the deal is done."

"It's done. I guess you're due for a bonus."

I went back to the room and packed. Kate never called. I stared at the phone, willing it to ring. She was smarter than that- sleeping with her boss. He was married even – what was she thinking? It was 4 PM. I called her office. Her secretary didn't recognize my voice. I asked if Kate was there. She said she wasn't. I asked if I could speak to her boss. She said they were together at a meeting. I checked out and went to Fred's room, ready for the trip back to Biotechna.

29

The six months between our scoring the Dewey financing and the FDA's rejection of the CXR application whipped by in a haze of happy hours and company outings. I had no work to do except keep some leftover animals alive. Fred Mathews was scouting some smaller biotechs that would be possible takeover or merger targets. It's the way it worked. After a small biotech has success with a compound like CXR. All the work for the past several years was focused on that one product, so there is no "next thing." Patents run out quickly, so a one-trick company can't stay independent long. If you don't have something in the pipeline, the thing to do is to acquire a company with promising compounds in early stages and start over. When you get enough product candidates you become a takeover target for one of the big pharmaceutical companies. Paying double the value of a small biotech company can be chump change to a large drug company, but to those invested in the biotech company, watching their wealth double overnight can be like hitting the lottery.

I got a $50,000 bonus after the financing deal went through and options on another 10,000 shares. The stock went as high as $84 in the weeks leading up to the FDA decision. Today, the shell of the Biotechna Company trades for about six cents a share when it trades at all. For less than thirty days after the stock had run-up from $3.50 to $84 on rumors of a favorable FDA decision, I had an on-paper net worth of more than 4 million dollars. Nearly all of my stock was restricted – I wouldn't have been able to sell it for months – but when I looked at my holdings statements, there it was, a four followed by six more digits- those six digits alone are more money than I'm likely to have again for a long, long time.

With the bonus I did have about $200,000 in cash on hand. I bought a boat- a thirty-two foot Bayliner. I was on the boat every day. The boat never left the dock, but I was on it every day. I didn't grow up with boats, and I didn't know anything about them except that rich people always seemed to have them. I felt rich, so I felt I needed a boat. I was stupid enough to buy a boat, but not stupid enough to take it out on open water – I could have killed somebody or gotten lost or something. The next level of rich is a plane. The peak of the rich-man stuff is the private jet. Fred Mathews was that rich, but he had nowhere to fly. Entry-level demonstration of excess wealth is a boat. Look at any marina on a day you think to yourself, "this would be a beautiful day to go out on a boat." If more than three percent of the boats are at sea, let me know, because I've never seen it. Except for the hardcore fishermen, nobody gets a boat and uses it.

During that golden period between the submission of the application and CXR's rejection, we had happy hour "meetings" at a local bar almost every night. Fred was enjoying the ride. Drinks were on the company. Fred would go in the bar's bathroom and come out with give-away eyes. Sometimes his pupils would fill his cornea so they would seem colorless. Sometimes the pupils were closed down so tight there would be no black in the center at all. No matter what the pupils and the irises were doing, the surrounding whites would be red. He would come out of the can either wired, and try to get some competition at the coin-op basketball game, or he would slither into a booth and put his head down on a damp tabletop, waking up later saying, "What I lose? An hour? Two?" His habits probably would have killed any one of us, but Fred kept it together. He rarely encouraged anyone else to use drugs. Smart of him – It was okay for him to be a burn-out, he was pretty much a figurehead, but he couldn't have the people that had to actually do the work be high all the time. You can criticize his judgment, but you've got to give him credit for his judgment.

Two days before the FDA decision was to be released, I called Kate at work. Somehow I was put through.

"Things are really happening here," I told her. "If the FDA approves CXR, I'll be retired within a year."

"That's great."

Something wasn't right with her. I didn't know what to expect when I called her. I didn't think she would talk to me at all. She wasn't short with me like she was angry or disinterested; she just talked sad and slow. Maybe I shouldn't have called her at all. I wanted to tell her what was going on. I thought maybe news of my impending success might make some difference. I needed to tell somebody; I needed to tell her. If she was pissed at me, she would have cut me off and hung up. If she wasn't, I would have expected a bit more excitement out of her, even if we had nothing to do with each other any more. Getting nothing at all made for a pretty awkward silence. I didn't think she was going to say anything if I didn't.

"What's wrong?"

"It's nothing."

"Kate, what's wrong."

"It's not your problem."

"It doesn't matter if it's my problem."

"I don't want to talk about it."

"With me? Or with anybody?"

"With you or anybody."

"All right. But if you change your mind, I'll listen."

"She's pregnant."

I guessed Kate meant her boss's wife was pregnant.

"When did that happen?"

"He told me two days ago."

"Are you doing O.K.?"

"He told me two days ago. We were on a plane, coming back from a weekend conference he took me to in San Francisco. The conference was an hour on Saturday afternoon, but he told his wife he had to leave Thursday and wouldn't be back until late Monday. He knew she was pregnant before we left, but he didn't tell me until the ride home."

"What did you do," I asked

"I kind of flipped out."

"What's 'kind of flipped out' mean?"

"I was beating the crap out of him. The flight attendants were looking for a doctor on board to give me sedatives from the medical kit. Fortunately, there were no armed marshals."

"Did you get in trouble?"

"The co-pilot talked me down. I told the flight attendants what he did to me, and she offered me an empty seat in first-class so we could be separated. He has a black eye. Told his wife he fell, and I'm sure she believes him."

"You still working there?"

"For now. I can't stay long. But he can't fire me so quick either, given the circumstances."

"That prick."

"I seem to attract them."

"Hey."

"Sorry. Look, I'm a little messed up about all this," she paused. "Can we talk about this some other time?"

"Do you want me to come down there?" You couldn't blame me for trying. "I got nothing going on until the FDA decision."

"No, don't come. Give me a call next week. Or maybe that's not such a good idea."

"I'll call. My dinner invitation is still on the table, you know."

"Don't try and take advantage of me on the rebound, Walter."

"Sorry."

"Call me next week," she said. "I'll think about dinner."

30

The FDA has modernized in recent years, but they still send drug approval and rejection decisions by telegram. Not FedEx, not email, not even a regular phone call – the FDA's decision to decline approval of CXR arrived by telegram. Fred still had the telegram in his hand when the CNBC reporter, live from the NASDAQ, let the world know that Biotechna was likely to be the "disaster *du jour.*"

By the end of the trading day, the news commentators were exchanging playful banter to clarify if *decimated* meant being reduced *by* one tenth of its original value or being reduced *to* one tenth of its original value. It is the former, but we were the latter. My paper $4 million was now a paper $400,000. Not bad, on paper, but I still couldn't get out, and Biotechna still had a ways to go down.

The FDA's letter that followed the telegram outlined why the panel had rejected the drug and what they would need to see in order for CXR to be approvable. Everything we knew about CXR told us there was no way it would perform the way FDA suggested it would have to. We were dead.

"The ride was cool, but our wave has crashed," Fred told us in the conference room after meeting with Michelson. The two of them had concurred that CXR, and therefore Biotechna, was finished.

"I'll tell the staff," Fred said. "I'll tell them to start looking for other jobs. I'll keep the lights on. Between the company's cash and some personal funds, I'll pay the salaries for three months, but then we'll have to shut her down."

I only had one lab tech that worked directly for me; he made about twenty bucks an hour. He said he'd stay on until the place closed – it was easy work, no work at all really – he would catch up on his reading and work the phones looking for a new job, letting them know he'd be available to start once the three months ran out.

I took a break from packing my office and called Kate. To not seem overanxious I let a week and two days pass from when I had last called her.

"She's not here." Unmistakably the same secretary from my visit.

"Do you know when she'll be in."

"She'll be back...Uhmm...never. She's left the company."

"Oh," I said.

"You're that Walter guy, right?" I was impressed she remembered. "Do you know why she left?"

"Are you asking me, or do you want to tell me?" I said.

"Hey, It's nobody's business she was sleeping with her boss. I'm not supposed to discuss it with anyone around here, but you're not around here and I'll take any outlet for gossip I can get."

"Glad I could help."

"Are you going to try and call her?"

"I *was* trying to call her."

"Will you call her at home?"

"I don't have her number."

"Maybe I do."

"Would you give it to me?"

"I can't give out an employees' home number."

"She's not an employee anymore."

"Hmmm...good point."

"Please."

"You're not going to get it that easy. Tell you what. Have two dozen red roses sent to me here with some gushy love note, and I'll give you her home number."

"Are you serious?"

"Are you?"

"All right, I'll send them. What's her number?"

"Not so fast. I get the roses, then you get the number."

"How do I know you'll give me the number?"

"You don't. You'll just have to trust me. And for doubting my integrity, I think the price just went up. Now it's two dozen red roses and a large teddy bear. Preferably one holding a heart."

Bitch.

"And see if you can make it one of those bears-holding-a-heart where you squeeze the heart and it plays music."

"Any song in particular?"

"Okay, *Mr. Sarcastic*. You want to play hardball? I'm seeing two dozen red roses on my desk next to a large white teddy bear holding a red heart pillow. When you press the pillow, the electronic tune of Elvis's "Love Me Tender" will be heard throughout the office. Any other questions?"

"I'll get right on it."

"You have 24 hours."

Including the flowers, vase, the Elvis singing-heart teddy bear, sales tax and the next-day delivery, but not including the dozen or so long-distance phone calls to locate an Elvis singing-heart teddy bear, Kate's phone number cost me almost $300. It was worth it.

31

I rehearsed my call to Kate for an hour before I had it down and was ready to dial. I wanted to get past about four levels of *and then she'll say... and then I'll say...* for every possible branch point in the conversation. I knew what I would say if she wanted to go back with her boss, if she found somebody new, if she wanted to see me right then, or anything that might come up including if she didn't want to talk to me at all. Once I had that down, I held the phone to my head and practiced different ways I could say "hello," including "hi," "how are you," "hello there," and toyed briefly with "wasssuppp." It was worse than the first time I tried to call her in high school. Back then it felt like getting it right was the most important thing in the world. Life was simpler then, so in a way calling her *was* the most important thing in the world. Now, life was more than just complicated, but getting it right still felt like the most important thing in the world. It was.

I was ready for just about anything. The only thing I wasn't ready for was what I got.

"Hello. This is Kate. Leave a message. Beeeeeeeeep."

I said what can only be described as "duh," hung up the phone and said "Fuck!"

About thirty seconds later, the phone rang.

"Hi, Walter. It's Kate."

"I just called you."

"I know. I recognized the 'duh' and got your number off the caller ID. You should hang up all the way before you yell 'fuck."

"Thanks for the tip. Sorry."

"I've been screening my calls. He called yesterday."

"Your boss?"

"My ex-boss. Ex-everything. I've been letting the machine pick up. He blabbered on about how sorry he was and how he wanted to make it up to me. If he had a video-phone all he would have seen was my middle finger."

None of this was on any of the scripts I had prepared in my head, so I winged it: "You doing okay?"

"Yeah. I got a new job – I start next week editing for KKN publishers. They have some big names, so it could be a good move. How are you doing? I saw your company's one-line blurb in the *Wall Street Journal* under 'Routs.'"

"Our company is finished. The head of the company is a rich ex-surfer dude with a ton of money, so he's keeping us all on the payroll a few weeks more, but without our drug getting approval, the company is worthless."

"What are you going to do?"

"I'm not sure yet. I called Underwood at Midstate. He's on Biotechna's board and knows what happened. He said he has something I might be interested in and told me to come down. I have no other prospects, so I'm going to see him."

After a few seconds she said, "I would like to see you."

"That was supposed to be my line," I said. "I'd like to see you too. Up here, or in the city?"

"Why don't we meet? One of the chefs from the Food Network just opened a place in that Indian casino- I saw it on TV and it looks pretty cool. Seeing how you just lost your job and I just got a new one, why don't you let me buy you dinner?"

"Hey, I'm not rich anymore, but I'm not broke. I still have some money. Dinner's on me- I owe you."

"Done."

"That was easy."

"That's it for easy," She said. "Anything else you're going to have to work hard for."

We set up to meet that weekend. The next day I went shopping for two outfits: a new suit for my meeting with Underwood, and something decent for my date with Kate.

32

Professor Underwood's office looked the same as it did the day I first met with him as an undergraduate. The first time I was there, he offered me a spot in his lab as an assistant. Now, I was back in the same office being offered a position in his department with my own lab. I'm sure the papers in the stack of journal articles I sat next to were different, but it was the same vertical file system: A large stack of articles with the most recently obtained ones on top, the oldest ones on the bottom. Scientists are reluctant to throw away scraps of papers and articles; even those who never in their lives have referred to a scientific doodle they made on a piece of scrap paper or ever referred to an ancient article that highlighted some obscure finding, still insisted on keeping a pile of articles and scrap paper within arms-reach because, "you never know."

"We were all hurt emotionally (and financially) when the FDA rejected Biotechna's CXR application," Underwood said. "But the timing of your unfortunate unemployment comes at an opportune time. I have been approached by Pharma to do some animal work on a promising drug."

"I'm not so sure I'm ready to work for another biotech just now."

"Working for Pharma would be more like working for a real pharmaceutical company, rather than a biotech. Pharma is the research arm of Biopic, which is the pharmaceutical arm of an even bigger multi-national corporation that makes everything from hand soap to dog food to turkey vaccines."

"Biopic is a pretty big drug company, right?" I had heard the name.

"They are the fifth largest developer of new pharmaceuticals in the US. They started developing new drugs about fifteen years ago.

Initially, they were a generic drug manufacturer – making other companies' drugs that had already been approved after the patents had expired. Biopics got a biotech company as part of some big takeover, expanded it, and called the biotech group Pharma. Pharma had a drug that turned out to be a hot cardiology drug - nothing like those cardiac stents or cholesterol drugs now, but huge at the time. Pharma continued with drug development and has done pretty well."

"Do you think it would be better to work for a pharmaceutical than a biotech?"

"You're getting ahead of yourself. You wouldn't be working for Pharma or Biopic. You would work for the university. I can get you appointed an assistant professor, junior faculty. It would be easy to sell to the chairman, because if you came on, you would get the Pharma project. It fully funds your position and would set up a new lab. Pharma has included several milestone awards in the deal, and when they start seeing data, they have offered the university several million dollars for the construction of a new lab wing."

"Interesting."

"Interesting? It's phenomenal. You would be the best-paid, best-equipped, new faculty member on campus. Plus, with the dollar amounts a project like this can bring to the university, you would be on the fast track for promotion."

"Best-paid, best equipped," I repeated.

"And Pharma has a speakers bureau. They'll send you to speak about their products at conferences – expenses paid plus a few thousand dollars in speakers' fees. I've done that kind of thing before, and I can tell you, the conferences are not in Binghamton."

"How come you're not taking it?" I asked Underwood.

"It's a five-year project. Don't mention this to the chairman, but I'm planning on retiring the year after next. Believe me, it's a sweet deal, and I'd take it if I could. But I won't be around to finish it, and, with this much at stake for the university, this has to be done right. Once the university hears about how valuable this project is for them, they will be very aggressive in making sure we keep Pharma happy."

He went on about Pharma's plans and how beneficial it would be for me, for the department, and for the university. He explained the relationship that would be set up between the university and the company and described the financial arrangements. As important a decision as it was, I couldn't stop thinking about Kate. I would be seeing her in three days. It *would* be better if I had a job when I saw her. Women prefer men with jobs, I suspect. I could work for Pharma, or at least on behalf of Pharma at Midstate. Underwood made it sound like they had all the protocols worked out, and knew what type of data they were looking for. All they needed was a university affiliated PhD to do the work for them. I could do that. It was the kind of work I trained for. The money was decent enough, and the sweeteners were pretty interesting. I saw myself taking Kate to conferences in the Caribbean, spending a few hours in a lecture hall, then enjoying expenses-paid, week-long vacations in the tropics.

Of course now I know how bad it all turned out. But when along the way could I have seen it coming and done something differently? I still would have met with the guys from Pharma. I still would have wanted the position. I still would have taken it. Even if I had read the Pharma contract more carefully, I probably still would have signed it. At the time, I thought I understood the 20-page contract. Actually, I did understand it. It was the implications of some of the easy-to-understand clauses that I didn't understand. And not anticipating what was to happen, I never would have questioned it.

My contract with the university was simpler. After the preliminaries it just said:

Walter Most, PhD, is hereby granted all rights and privileges of Assistant Professor of Applied Physiology. This contract is contingent upon Dr. Most remaining compliant with his agreement with Pharma Corp.

I signed them both.

I would see Kate that weekend and meet with the Pharma people Monday to go over the details of my new lab.

It was the beginning of the end.

PART 5

PHARMA

33

My new lab was down the opposite hallway from Underwood's in the Old Research Building. Nobody in the department had been quite sure what kind of work Dr. Fine had been doing with the baby pigs, but when the university saw the money my contract with Pharma would bring in, he was relocated. It took a few weeks for all the lab materials to come in from the supply companies, and a month for the construction team to complete the renovations, but when they were finished, my lab looked a century ahead of Underwood's. Everything in his lab was dull, rusted, and dinged; everything in mine was shiny and sleek. My lab had been redone with new plasterboard painted lab-coat white, a new drop ceiling, and full-spectrum lighting that made the place shine. Underwood's lab – really all the research labs at Midstate - still had layer upon layer of different colors of peeling paint over cinder block walls. Strewn about the mismatched tables in Underwood's lab were laboratory notebooks where animals' weights, drug protocols and the like were entered by hand. The only computer in Underwood's lab was a pre-Windows machine used solely for data entry and analysis.

Pharma's grant provided a state-of-the-art computer system with a wireless network of flat-panel touch screen computers. The protocols would be sent from Pharma over the internet for execution in my lab. When any animal's cage was opened, its profile would appear on the computer screen and included to which treatment group they belonged and where each animal was in the study. Each rat's food and water intake was measured electronically and sent to the computers, and when the rats were placed on the scale, the reading was automatically included in the on-screen profile. The system itself probably only saved about 15 minutes of work per day, but it was the coolest looking thing going, and during the first few weeks people from other departments would pop in just to look at the equipment. They didn't know if the space-age gadgetry could help them with their own research efforts, but they all knew they wanted it.

Pharma would design all the studies and forward all the protocols. The raw data would be sent back to Pharma for analysis. I hated doing the statistical analysis, so I didn't mind. The connection between my lab and Pharma meant they could take care of all that.

The people from Pharma said they didn't want me to have to rely on graduate students, so my contract included a lab technician to perform the hands-on work of the experiments. Before the first protocols arrived she didn't have much to do but make sure the electronics worked and the animals were fed. She was always moving around the lab, reminding me of the people in the background you see in medicine commercials, the ones working behind the doctor who is alerting the viewers to important clinical findings that can help them live better. (Often hyping cures for problems they didn't even know they had, cures with side effects no sane person would risk.) Most real labs looked like Underwood's, but most of them didn't have the funding mine got from Pharma. Any of the other professors would have killed for my air-handling system. Most rodent labs smelled like an unattended men's room on a hot day, mine had a light cedar-chip odor you could sometimes pick up in the house of someone who has a well cared for hamster.

My most recent attempt at another first date with Kate was perfect. After dinner we went for a walk by the water and talked about what had happened to us during the years since we had last been together. She laughed when I was startled by a boat's air horn, and we caught each other's eyes. We went close to kiss. I was hoping for a long, slow one, but she pulled back quickly.

"I don't know where I want this to go," she said. "But I know I don't want it to go anywhere fast."

"I understand," I said, though it didn't mean I was happy about it.

We walked the rest of the bay path holding hands. I kissed her goodnight at her car and we agreed to see each other again, but didn't make plans just then. I had no doubt then that I still loved her; I have no doubts about that now.

Part of my job included giving one ninety-minute lecture per week. It was a 100 level applied biophysiology course. All science majors had to take the introductory course. Those who were interested in the topic were generally ahead of the 100-level course depth already; those who were not interested only care about passing, and most of those people took the course pass/fail, which was supposed to take some of the pressure off the students and let them get the most out of the class. What it did was allow students to put in the least possible effort required to get a passing grade. I know. I was there.

As little as the students cared about the subject in general, they cared about my lectures even less. Most everyone had some connection to test files, and all the students knew, just as I had known when I was in the same lecture hall for the same course, that the final exams were constructed from question banks, so the content of my lectures was irrelevant as far as their grades were concerned. About the only thing that could have generated interest during my lectures was some announcement about changes in the exam date or location. Otherwise, it was the same every week: 20% asleep by the end of the hour, 20% with apparent interest, and 60% just marking time. It worked out okay; I didn't expect much from them, they didn't expect much from me. That each of them (or their families) was paying almost $30,000 a year for the privilege of sitting in those seats was comical.

It wasn't until near the end of the semester that Pharma forwarded the first experimental protocols and delivered the study medications to my lab. It didn't change my routine much, it just gave my lab tech something to do that looked more like research.

I saw Kate two more times before winter break, always meeting on neutral ground. Each time we were together the hand holding time got a little longer, the kissing a little heavier. I thought things were going pretty well. I tried to talk her into coming up to Midstate after finals, but she wouldn't go for it.

"Why don't you come to New York next time. There's more going on here, you have to admit."

"Better than ten-cent wing night?"

"I'm sure we could find something to do."

"It's a long drive," I said. "I don't think I could really drive down, have dinner and drive back."

"I'm sure we could find somewhere you could stay."

I took that, erroneously as it would turn out, to mean I could stay at her place. After we hung up, I couldn't get her out of my head. It had been a while since I had been with anyone, and longer still since I had been with Kate. I was alone in a college town, and all I could see when I closed my eyes was some memory of Kate. I took matters into my own hands.

34

Even though I was research faculty with an important grant, I felt like I had fewer responsibilities than I did when I was an undergrad in Underwood's lab. Pharma sent the medications in pre-measured syringes. The study protocols were all worked out on the computer. The lab tech weighed, fed and watered the animals. She administered the drugs and on the designated days drew blood samples. She packed the samples on dry ice and arranged for them to be shipped to Pharma for analysis. The data automatically found its way to the computer system; all the blood test results were posted on the internet at a site accessible only from Pharma and from my lab.

The first project was a dose-finding project. Rats got different amounts of the study drug, and the effects of each dose were analyzed. For most compounds you get a small effect for a small dose, a little more effect from a larger dose, and a larger effect from a still larger dose. At some point you can keep increasing the dose but the effect doesn't get any greater. The side effects can also be dose related. The idea is to find the dose where you get the most effect with the fewest side effects. For some drugs there is no dose adequate enough to yield some benefit without also causing harm. These drugs never get developed unless the disease they are aimed at is particularly terrible. Vomiting, abdominal pain, and anemia are unfortunate but acceptable side effects of a drug treating cancer, but are unacceptable in a drug for hay fever.

The week we (OK, my lab tech) finished the first trial, I received three files from Pharma. The first was an elaborate Excel spreadsheet compiling the data from the trial with a detailed statistical analysis and data summary. The first line of the second file was the title of a research paper, under the title was my name, and what followed was a twelve-page paper including the introduction, methods, results, discussion, conclusions and reference sections. The third file was a letter from Tyler Stanley, my contact at Pharma, asking me to review the included research paper, and then a list of several academic journals to which he suggested I submit the article for publication. There were no printers in the lab, so I read the manuscript on the screen. It *was* good. I called Tyler Stanley.

"Walter, how you doing, man," Tyler said. I had only met him once, when he brought me the contract, but he came off like he was catching up with a best bud from college.

"I'm all right. I'm calling to find out the deal with the files I was sent."

"Did you have a problem opening them?"

"No, they got here fine."

"Good. What can I do for you?"

"I was just trying to find out what the story is."

He paused. "No problem-o Walter. They are your data and a suggested paper for submission."

"What do you mean, 'suggested?'"

"Did you read the paper, Walter?"

"Yes."

"What did you think?"

I paused. "It's good, I guess."

"Just good?"

"Okay, it's very good." Most people outside science, as well as most people inside, would be unwilling or unable to get past page one, but as far as a research paper discussing a drug experiment in rats goes, it was very good.

"So go with it then."

"Go with it?"

"Yeah. Submit it to one of the journals. If you want to write your own paper, you can. It will take you a few weeks, then you will have to send it to us for approval, then you'll have to revise it, then we'll have to approve the revisions. It will take a few months to get out essentially the same information, but you can do it that way if you feel better about it. Frankly, most people we work with stick with the papers we help them generate. Fewer hassles."

"You've done this before."

"Walter, this *is* how we do it. You like writing the research papers?"

"It's part of the job."

"I know Walter, but isn't the real job the lab work?"

"I guess so."

"Division of labor. You do the science. We have full time statisticians doing the analysis. You enjoy working with the statistical software packages, Walter?"

"Who does?"

"We also have a cadre of writers who specialize in this kind of writing. Their writing is a hell of a lot more readable than your average science geek's. Know what I mean?"

It was true, most researchers, even the most prolific, have little grasp of grammar and less sense of style.

"So we find this is the best way to proceed," Tyler continued. "You do the science, let the math people do the stats, let the word people write the papers. The information is the same stuff you would have communicated if you wrote the paper – it's your science- so don't worry about taking the credit for the paper. Our writers are under contract. They are paid well, so don't feel bad for them. Read the paper and make sure it fits what you would say about the work you did. If you can stand behind it, then there is nothing wrong with your name on the paper. Believe me, Walter, this is how it's done."

"Okay, Tyler. Thanks."

It had the feel of a hard sell, but he made some sense. It was a lot easier than going through the publication process from scratch, especially with the extra step of needing to get Pharma's approval for everything I did. I was guaranteed a job at the university for the five years of my Pharma contract, but after that I was subject to the university's 'up-or-out' policy. If I didn't get promoted through the academic ranks, I would lose my position- who knew where Dr. Fine and his piglets ended up? The promotion cycle was seven years, and I would have to have 50 points by then. Each department had a list of journals and points associated with each journal. Most of the journals were designated as two-pointers, so, in order to be promoted, the average assistant professor needed 25 publications in the seven years. It was purely weight based. There was no measure of quality of any individual publication; all that mattered was the number of papers published. If Pharma was going to write the papers for me, promotion would be no problem.

I read the 'suggested' paper that Pharma had sent one more time. It did read well, and it did say all the things I would try to say if I was writing the thing up myself. I typed up a quick email cover letter, attached Pharma's version of the paper, and sent it off to the first journal on Pharma's recommended list. Everything was done online. My university considered it a two-point journal. The review process usually takes two months, but my paper was accepted for publication in two weeks. The journal's editors requested no revisions. They would run it as is.

When I read the acceptance letter from the journal I remember thinking: One down, 24 to go.

35

Within nine months of that first paper being published, I had ten manuscripts either accepted for publication or under consideration by one of the major journals. I had six more years to get to the 25 that would qualify me for tenure, so I was way ahead. At that point I could have stopped taking Pharma's manuscripts as my own and started doing it the right way, and I would have had no problem getting the needed 25. But why? What's the difference who picks out the words, right? Besides, rocking the boat probably would have upset the people at Pharma, and my contract with the university was contingent upon my relationship with Pharma.

By then all I would do was skim the manuscripts Pharma sent, and occasionally I didn't even do that. I would just make sure the electronic file I was forwarding was indeed the manuscript and not some other communication. I knew a guy once who spent months preparing a manuscript, a week polishing the cover letter, and most of a day getting the envelope set. It was going to some big journal like *Science* or *Nature,* I don't remember which, but it was one of the majors. Turns out that in his beautiful envelope with his perfect cover letter was a purchase order for cedar chips and a copy of his cellular phone bill. He found the manuscript on his desk after the mail had been picked up. He got a call from the journal's editor, telling him there must have been some mistake, but also told him to not bother sending the manuscript. Something about how if he couldn't even keep his papers straight... I never made any changes to the papers Pharma sent me, but I always made sure I was sending the journals what I thought I was sending them.

Things were going well with Kate. I was seeing her every other weekend, either in New York City or up at Midstate. We agreed we wouldn't see anyone else. She decided and made me agree, that we wouldn't sleep together for a year from our most recent try at our first date. I didn't like that, but I didn't want to press my luck. In high school she was out of my league. In college I could have done it right, but I fucked it up. I've known since the first time we spent some time together she was the one, and now, if I had a real chance, I wouldn't lose her again. Don't get me wrong, I wanted to sleep with her- more so every time I saw her – but unlike in college, and probably for the first time in my life, I would try to balance a moment's pleasure against a lifetime's satisfaction.

Pharma provided regular speaking engagements. About once per month, Pharma set me up with a carousel of slides, round-trip tickets, a hotel, and some spending money, and sent me to a city that had a medical school to educate the academics about what was to be coming soon from Pharma. It was their way of building a support base, a group of doctors who would then promote Pharma's products in medical schools, which would result in a group of new physicians who would start prescribing what Pharma had to offer when they graduated. Everyone knew that doctors get in the habit of prescribing certain medications – if they learn to use something in medical school, they will probably use it throughout their careers. Doctors are resistant to change, even when what's new is proven to be better; it takes years to replace the old favorites. I was a missionary for Pharma. They sent me out to spread their fertilizer with hopes that beautiful sales would grow.

"Have you ever been to Hawaii?"

Tyler Stanley called with another promotional talk for me to deliver.

"No."

"There's an internal medicine meeting out there next week. We offered them a speaker for a special session. If you're busy, I can give it to someone else, but the people in Vegas said you did a nice job, so I thought we'd offer you this one too."

"Can I bring a guest?"

"Sure. We can get two tickets. The spending money has to be the same, I'm afraid."

"That's fine," I said. Actually, it was awesome. "I'm not sure if she can get away- can I get back to you?"

"By the end of the week. I'll get the tickets. Hawaii's awesome – we had our annual meeting there last year. You're going to love it."

I called Kate that night.

"Yes, I want to go," she said, "I just finished a manuscript, and I have some time coming."

"I swear it's a budget thing," I told her, "but they will only get us one room."

"That's okay," she said.

"Does that mean the year thing is…"

"We agreed not to sleep together for a year. I think you know the difference between not *sleeping* together and not sleeping together."

"Hawaii's pretty romantic. I don't know if I'll be able to stand that," I said.

"If you don't want me to come, I'll under…"

"No. We're going. I'll tell them to get two tickets from Kennedy, and I'll meet you at the airport."

I hadn't seen Kate naked since the beginning of college. In fact, in the time we had been dating again, I hadn't seen more of her than what was left uncovered by khaki shorts and a t-shirt. On the beach in Honolulu, I tried, unsuccessfully, not to gawk at her in her bikini. When we talked, I always started looking at her eyes, but two or three words later, my gaze would go down to her breasts, which had the perfect balance of exposed and covered in her two-piece. From there, if she didn't clear her throat or make some other gesture to try and get my roving peepers back to her eye level, I'd run down her ribs to what I think is my favorite part of her, just at the soft spot below where the last rib ends. If she didn't stop my visual survey with some protest, it proceeded. From the spot below her ribs my eyes followed the contour towards her navel, and then either curved out towards the string whose knot was holding her suit bottom on, or go in towards the fine trail of hair, no more than five hairs wide, that started just below her bellybutton and went south to disappear at her bikini line.

"Did you hear anything I just said, Walter?" She was smiling.

"Yeah...you were just saying how the thing that...Um...no."

"Hold it together, mister. You got two months left on the deal, and I'm starting to wonder if you're going to make it."

"Being on vacation doesn't count for anything?" I asked. There was no visible evidence of what was on my mind, but I could feel a pulse in my bathing suit and my thoughts would be telegraphed in a moment if I couldn't clear my head.

"*I'm* on vacation," she said. "This is a business trip for you."

"Fine." I rolled on my back and stared at the passing clouds. Each cloud looked like some sexual position. Sixty days.

That night was worse. I had a talk to give at the medical school the next morning, and I couldn't sleep. We were a foot apart on this oversized bed. I was stroking her hair, and she fell asleep. All I could think about was wanting to be *with* her. I drifted off and woke up maybe two dream-strokes away from messing my pajamas. I went to brush my teeth to make the feeling pass and then went back to bed.

"What's wrong," she asked.

"Nothing."

She kissed me, and I kissed her back. Hard. She came up on top of me and I slipped my hand under her top. She pressed herself into me. My hand slid down her back and into her bottoms, following the curve and reaching between her thighs. She let out a heavy exhale when my fingers brushed up against some hair. She pushed harder into me then jumped off.

"Walter, we can't"

"You sure?" The pulse in my groin was back.

"It's how it has to be Walter."

"I understand." I didn't.

It was 6 AM. "I'm going to start getting ready.

The shower was made of California-glass blocks. From inside the shower you could see silhouettes of what was in the rest of the bathroom. I was soaping up when the bathroom door opened.

Kate stood in front of the shower door. I watched through the glass as her distorted figure took her top off, then her panties. I pushed the door enough to release the magnet that was holding it shut. She walked towards the shower, opened the door, and came in. My eyes fixed on hers. I kissed her, put my hands on her back, and slid down to my knees. I drank from between her legs, harder and faster both from the excitement and to keep from drowning. I felt the muscles in the back of her thighs tighten and felt her pull my head in towards her. She shuddered, released my head, and again I was aware of the water. She pulled me up by the shoulders, smiled an evil smile, and kissed me. First on my mouth, then my neck, my chest, and then...

We didn't speak until we were toweling off after.

"Does this mean the deal..." I started.

"No. Same deal. According to Clinton, we didn't have sexual relations, so we're still good. One of us might have had sex, you would have to ask him which one, but I'm certain that according to the former President, *we* didn't have sex *together*."

"Could we not have sex again?" I asked.

"Not for two more months. I couldn't send you out to give a talk like that. I took one for the team."

"That's what you call that?"

She smiled. "Go get dressed."

My presentation went well. Kate was right. I don't think I could have kept my mind on the topic if I hadn't released some pressure. As a trade-off, however, my oral explorations left a bit of callus under my tongue, which I think left some of the audience wondering if I had some sort of a speech impediment.

36

A couple weeks after our Hawaii trip, Kate came up to visit and met me at the lab. I was looking at a new manuscript, my twelfth from Pharma, which I had just received. The email that came with the paper said they would be starting Phase I human trials with the drug soon. Tyler Stanley's note thanked me for the work I had done so far, suggested there was plenty to still be done, and indicated that there would be even more opportunity for speaking engagements once the human trials started. He wanted to know if I would be available for another trip the following month. With Pharma covering all expenses and me netting about two grand for a trip, I would be available.

"I'm going to look at the animals while you finish up," Kate said.

I pretended to review the manuscript on the computer screen for a few more minutes, but after Kate appeared, I could no longer make any sense of it. I closed the file and forwarded it to the journal Pharma recommended along with the cover letter that Pharma had sent along. It has since been published, and I still have never read the whole thing. After I received the *successfully sent* message, I joined Kate.

"Your lab's a lot nicer than Underwood's," she said. "Is he jealous?"

"No. He helped set it up. He's retiring next year anyway. Some of the other faculty are pretty jealous though."

"Can I hold one?"

She loved animals, even the lab rats, and I thought back to her playing with Paulina in Underwood's lab.

"Take one from that rack," I told her. "They are from last month's experiment. They are just hanging around until Pharma picks them up." Besides providing the study designs, drugs, a lab tech, and the finished manuscripts, Pharma also arranged to have the rats collected after the experiments. It was better than having to spend a day killing them.

"Hey fella," she said, holding a rat under its forepaws with her thumb and index finger. She and the rat were nose to nose.

"I don't know how they drag those things around," I said, pointing to the rodent's disproportionate testicles.

"Maybe you should get them little rat jock straps."

"I'll call Pharma."

She put that rat into her palm and started stroking its back.

"What's that?" she said, flipping the rat over.

"What?"

"This."

She took my hand and pressed my fingers into the rat's belly. It was lumpy. The lab work was done by my lab tech, so I hadn't handled a rat in almost a year and never would have noticed. The rat's belly was lumpy.

"What do you think it is?" she asked.

"Feels like some kind of tumor. I don't know. I never felt that before."

"When my Golden was 14, it started getting lumps like this," she said. "It was cancer. He was dead a month later."

I took another rat out of a cage from the same rack – no lumps. A second – no lumps. The third I picked up had the lumps bigger than those in the rat Kate was holding. I checked them all. Out of the 36 rats in the rack, eight had tumors.

"You think it could be the drug you've been testing?" she asked.

Of course it could have been, but I couldn't be sure. This was the first batch of rats that wasn't killed right after the experiments. There was no way to know what might have happened to rats we tested earlier.

"I don't know. Their experiment only ended a few weeks ago, and they weren't exposed to the drug for that long. It seems kind of fast for it to be the drug, but I guess it's possible."

"What are you going to do?"

"I have a friend over in the Biology Department. I'll ask him to do some pathology to see what kind of tumor it is. I'll call the Pharma people next week."

"What if it *is* the drug?" she asked.

"If the drug causes cancer, they might have to stop development."

"Would you be out of a job?"

"Pharma is a big company," I said. "I'm sure they have other products in development we could test for them – I don't know. I've had a lot of manuscripts published, so I would hope the university would let me stay even if Pharma pulled my contract. Without Pharma, though, I'd be back at a junior faculty's regular salary. No more Hawaii trips." I raised my eyebrows toward her at the thought of our Hawaii trip.

I put the last rat back in its cage, locked up the lab, and took Kate out for dinner. It could have been the drugs, but it could have been a bad batch of rats too. Those lab rats are so over-bred, you never know when a tumor-causing genetic defect is going to be unmasked. Tumors *did* spontaneously break out among batches of lab rats. Certain viruses that wouldn't bother a wild rat could wipe out a whole population of lab-bred rats. Still, it was hard to believe it could be anything but the drug. If it were just a genetic predisposition, would all those tumors appear at once? I was curious, but with Kate up for the weekend, it would wait until Monday.

37

"Hepatocellular carcinoma."

"You're shitting me."

"Nope," Mike Winters said. "Hepatocellular carcinoma. A real strange kind also. Look."

Mike Winters was a pathophysiology professor. When I was a freshman, he was a junior, and he lived in my dorm. He was one of the Hearts and Euchre geeks that stayed up all night playing cards. There were eight of them who would play just about every day in the kitchenette, passing potato chips, Doritos, and Dr. Pepper (no beer in the public areas), playing cards all night with an intensity only matched at a World Series of Poker event. No money changed hands – at least not over the table. It wasn't about that.

Only five of the eight came back the next year; three failed out. Mike, like me, also wanted to go to medical school but didn't make it. In an effort to improve his study habits, he became an RA the next year and broke up card games instead of playing. When he didn't get into medical school, he also went to graduate school, and now he was on faculty in the Biology Department. The other four of his card buddies got an off-campus apartment together, and I never saw or heard from them again.

Mike set up some slides on a double-headed microscope so we could look at the tissue samples together and so he could use a pointer to show me what to look at. I hadn't seen microscope slides in a long time, so it took a few minutes for my eyes to regain stereovision. My junior-year cellular physiology course was a distant memory, but the first slide he showed looked all right to me.

"I thought I'd show you a normal rat liver sample first," he started, using his joystick to direct a glowing blue arrow around the slide. "See how the architecture of the cells is regular, repeating patterns of concentric rings. Except where you see a big blood vessel or a duct, one section looks the same as any other."

"I see."

"Now look at your rat's liver."

He changed the slide and we looked through the viewfinder. He didn't join in with the pointer right away because he wanted me to get the full effect.

"This doesn't look like the other one."

"What do you see?" he asked me.

"It looks sloppy. It looks like a litter box full of turds."

"I've never heard it described that way, but that's accurate enough. Look at these clumps of dark-staining cells – the turds- these are the cancer cells. See how the cells are different than the normal cells, and how they don't organize themselves the way they are supposed to? It's pretty impressive. Most people say it looks like a lawn full of crabgrass, but turds will do."

"What causes this?"

"If I knew what caused cancer, I'd be rich."

"Any ideas about what caused it in this rat?"

"The pattern is most consistent with an induced cancer. More the kind you see after chronic hepatitis or with toxins."

"I'm concerned it might be a toxin."

"Part of the drug experiments you're running?"

"Maybe, I don't know."

"You might want to keep it quiet until you know more," he said.

"What do you mean?"

"No company wants to hear its drug causes cancer. See if you can get more information."

"Thanks."

When people study cancer epidemiology, one thing they look for is a dose-response curve. The idea is that the more of a toxin you are exposed to, the more likely you should be to develop the cancer. The relationships aren't perfect and plenty of tumors that looked like they had a clear cause turned out to be only due to chance. Some tumors have so many contributing causes that it is hard to pinpoint any one particular exposure as *the* cause.

The rats from my lab could have come out of an epidemiology textbook. No rat in the groups that received the two lowest doses of the drug had any tumors. A couple in the third highest dose group had tumors, and all but one in the high dose group had the tumors. The only thing left to prove it would be to take a fresh group of cancer-free rats and expose them to the drug and see if the tumors appeared.

I didn't know what to do. Pharma would soon pick up the rats- it was a fluke that these rats were kept in my lab as long as they were. Had the people at Pharma seen this kind of tumor before? They were starting the human trials, so I figured they must not have. I called Tyler Stanley.

38

"He's in a meeting right now," Tyler Stanley's secretary at Pharma said. "May I take a message?"

"Ask him to call Walter Most at Midstate- it's important."

I went into the lab while I waited for Tyler to call back. It was still a beautiful rat lab. No rust on the cages, bright white walls, full spectrum, no smell.

The lab tech was injecting an array of animals on the back left wall of the lab.

"What are you working on," I asked.

"Protocol 17. It's on the computer. Today is a treatment day," she said.

"Can I see the protocol?"

"It's on the computer, Dr. Most."

"Can I get a hard copy to look over?"

"Dr. Most, you know this is a paperless lab. It's right there on the screen."

I hadn't had much reason to do any hands-on work in the lab. I was no different than any of the other professors. Underwood spent very little time with the animals. Steve and Martin and I did all the work, and now there was a new crop of graduate students doing what would be the last batch of experiments for him. We presented the data to Underwood, who helped us write up the results and come up with the next step in our line of study. I had it even easier than Underwood- Pharma developed the protocols, the lab techs did the hands-on work, Pharma analyzed the data and even provided the write-ups. All I had to do was give it my PhD seal of approval. It was such a good gig I didn't give it much thought. If it weren't for those damn rats with liver tumors, I would have been planning my next speaking trip instead of trying to figure out what exactly it was I had been doing for the past year.

I fiddled with the computers. All the protocols and all the data were indeed right there on the screen. You could highlight an animal and get a graphical display of weight, urine output, metabolic markers, or any other piece of data that had been collected as part of the experiment. Rats that were harvested (killed) had red circles with slashes through them on the days they completed their usefulness.

There was no printer in the lab, so I tried to print out the protocols on the printer in my office. It was like any other computer. Under the *File* menu I selected *Print*.

UNABLE TO FIND PRINTER. RETRY OR CANCEL?

There was a combination fax-printer in the lab. I looked for it in the computer's control panel. Then I looked for a modem to send it to a fax.

"So you can't even send a fax?"

"No. The computers are on Pharma's server. There is no modem and no printer. You can't even select the text and put it in an email. It's very secure."

"What if I needed to print something?"

"You have a printer in your office."

I was starting to feel like one of those simpleton bosses they portray in those situation comedies- the guy who is in charge, although it's never clear how he got to be in charge. The office is really run by an assistant who always gets the boss to see it her way, and the boss just repeats what the assistant suggests as though it were his idea. It was funnier on TV than it was in my lab, and I remembered the lab tech didn't work for me, she was provided by Pharma.

I went back to my office and got a CD. I put it in the slot of the tower. The lab tech just shook her head. The computer made no sound – none of that whirring you get when you put a disk in a computer. Nothing.

I pulled up a protocol page, opened the *File* menu and selected *Save*.

Nothing.

I opened the *Save As* menu. The box opened, but there was no choice of locations to save a file.

"You know," the lab tech startled me, "there is no disk drive, Dr. Most."

"I did not know that. Thank you."

I pushed the button to get my disk out. Nothing happened. There was no drive behind the slot, so there was nothing connected to the eject button to push my disk out. Now the blank disk was in there like jammed change in a soda machine.

I went back to my office, got my digital camera, and stood in front of the screen snapping pictures of each page. Protocols, rat data, whatever- I photographed them. I was just trying to prove that I could generate a hardcopy of the information if I chose to. I filled my compact flash card.

"Ha!" I said, showing the tech how I beat the system.

Photographing the pages was a big mistake. When I went back to the lab, the lab tech hurried to end a cell-phone conversation. I can't say for sure who it was, but right after she hung up, the phone in my office rang. It was Tyler Stanley.

"Hey, Dr. Most. I got a message you called. What can we do for you?"

"I had some questions about the drug."

"Shoot."

"Have you noticed any side effects in any of your other trials?"

"Like what?"

"Anything, really." I couldn't decide if I should show all my cards at once. The lab tech made me suspicious.

"It appears safe. All your data and the other data we have collected from the other sites tell us we may have a winner here. The human trials are starting, you know."

"I know. That's really good." When a company announced it had a product candidate that was making the jump from animal to human trials, especially a drug like this where the market would be measured in billions, the stock price would shoot up.

"Good?" he said. "It could be awesome. Your data was instrumental in preparing the human protocols, and we're expecting more essential information from your lab over the next few months to direct the Phase I and II trials. I meant to ask you, are you available to present the preliminary data at a scientific convention in St. Thomas? It's next week."

"Uh..." Damn. St. Thomas. He was good. "I may be. But I wanted to ask you if you had any reports of unusual tumors in any of the lab subjects that received the higher doses of the drug?"

"None. As far as we can tell, the drug is safe – at least in the lab rats. Now we have to show it works in people."

"Some of the animals in my lab have developed liver tumors, and from the way the tumors appeared, it looks like it is a result of treatment with the drug."

"I can assure you that I haven't heard anything about any tumors from any of the other investigators," Tyler said. I'll tell you what, let me look into it, and I'll let you know. We don't want to expose any people to the drug unless we're sure it's safe."

He was a salesman, and I was sold. It sounded like they were going to look into it, and what more could I ask? Maybe it was a fluke. It was hard to be sure in a scientific sense. Pharma had spent millions of dollars on development, so I couldn't expect them to abandon it on the basis of a mere possibility. St. Thomas sounded good.

"I can't go," Kate said. "I have a manuscript to finish."

"I don't want to go without you."

"It's February, and the trip is to the Caribbean. *I'd* go without *you*."

"I'll think about it."

"What's wrong?" she asked. She could always tell when I was preoccupied.

"I'm just wondering about those rats. Pharma said they haven't heard of any problems with tumors. Tyler said the drug has been under development for years – if it were the drug, he was sure they would have seen something by now."

"How sure are you it's the drug?" she asked.

"It's hard to be sure, but it seems like too much of a coincidence for it to be anything else."

"What are you going to do?"

"I called them yesterday. They said they would look into it. I'm just concerned that if they pull the plug on the project, I'll be out of a job again."

"Well, if the drug causes cancer, you don't want them to give it to people, do you?"

To be honest, I hadn't been thinking about it from that perspective. Even after Kate said it that way, I still was more concerned about my employment than the possibility of a liver tumor in some faceless person of the future.

"No," I said after a long pause. "That would be terrible."

"So see what happens after they look into it."

"I will."

Outside the door to my lab the next morning were ten empty ventilated cardboard boxes. The lab tech was unloading boxes of fresh rats into the cages. Each new animal was checked in on the computer, weighed, and set up with fresh food and water.

"What's going on?" I asked.

"They sent us the new batch of rats. Tyler Stanley called and said you were concerned about some irregularities and wanted the animals analyzed. He told me to have them ready for shipping this morning. They were exchanged for these new ones. I thought you would have known." She held up one of the pups. "Don't you love them as babies."

The body of the baby rat was the size of her thumb, the tail was as long as its body. The rat's hair was pure white; age and repeated contact with rat urine hadn't yellowed it yet. The ears, nose and eyes were pink. The nose nervously sniffed about her hand, seeking anything familiar in the constantly changing surroundings of a lab rat in transit. Seeing nothing familiar, the rat peed. Now there was something to remember her hand by.

"Yes," I said. "Very cute. Where did the other rats go?"

"I don't know where they go. They just picked them up like all the other times."

I went to my office and called Tyler.

"What's up with the rats?" I asked.

"I told you we were going to look into it. When the rats get here, we'll have them autopsied and see what the problem might be. Have you decided about St. Thomas?"

I looked at the gray-brown snow heaped up on the walkways behind the research building. Even if we were starting a new project, there would be nothing for me to do at the lab – my lab tech did all the work. "Yeah, I'm available."

"Great. I'll get the slides to you today so you can review the talk. I'll book you a room for three nights. Will you be traveling with someone?"

"No."

"Too bad. By the time you get back, we should have some more information on those rats of yours."

I wanted to believe him, so I did. They had sent for the rats because they wanted to get the answer quickly. They sent new animals because they believed my rats were going to prove to be an anomaly, and the work needed to go on. I had reviewed the press release where Pharma announced it was recruiting physicians' offices as sites for the human trials of the drug. Four days in the Caribbean mid winter would be a good place to wait for the results.

The slides arrived by overnight carrier. I went to Macy's and bought a new bathing suit. In a couple days I'd be off to St. Thomas. It would be my last trip as a representative of Pharma. No additional offers would be made to me, and a few months after my return I would served with a subpoena and a restraining order preventing me from discussing anything regarding Pharma's proprietary information with anyone.

St. Thomas was awesome and only could have been better if Kate had been able to go- four days in the sun with one hour of public speaking. The shit started towards the fan when I got back.

39

I called Tyler the Friday I got back from St. Thomas.

"Any results?" I asked.

"Several of them had tumors, but our genetics people say you had a bad batch of rats. They are all from one line, and our gene guys say they were predisposed to the liver tumors. It was just bad luck, not the drug. At most, they thought it could have been some quirk interaction between the genetic defect and the drug, but not the drug itself. We haven't seen any other problems, so I think we're all right."

I couldn't argue with him, and I didn't have the rats with tumors anymore. Tyler was a salesman, not a scientist, but he sounded like he knew what he was talking about.

"Thanks for checking," I said. "I guess we'll keep going with the current protocol."

It would have been easier to just let it go. Tyler said it wasn't the drug. I had a good job, a good lab, and Kate. Why push it? Even if I still thought it was the drug, I didn't have to pursue it any further. I found something suspicious, and I reported it. Shouldn't that have been the end of my responsibility? Things were going well, and I could have just let it slide. I let stuff slide all the time until then. Why did I start caring about the truth then?

It could have been a bad batch of rats – I never heard of that before, but it must it must have been a possibility. It wasn't right to just assume Tyler was lying. Even if the drug did cause the liver tumors, it was only in the high-dose animals that the lesions came out like popcorn. Maybe it was one of those saccharine-like effects where, yes, it does cause problems, but you'd have to have something like four-dozen cans of diet soda every day for so many years to be at a significant risk.

Even though it had been a long time since I believed the mission of scientists was to find the truth –the point of science is to find the truth, but the practice of scientists has more to do with funding and tenure and publication and prestige than it does with the truth- but there had to be *some* things where finding the truth is what mattered. I didn't want to risk losing my lab, my speaking tour, my publication fast track or any of the other benefits that came from my association with Pharma, but, at the same time, I couldn't stop thinking that I knew what had caused the tumors in the rats.

Tyler Stanley could say they believed it was not the drug, and I could let it go and say I believed it too. In the end, it didn't matter what any of us believed: Either the drug caused the tumors or it didn't. For reasons I *still* don't fully understand, I just had to know.

Figuring it out wouldn't be too hard. Get a bunch of rats, give them the drug, watch them for a couple months, and then check their livers. The obstacles were that I didn't have the drug, and I couldn't do the work in my lab. My Pharma-hired lab tech would certainly rat me out with Pharma if I started doing something suspicious, and the whole lab was hard wired back to Pharma, so they would figure it out soon enough if something was being done off protocol. I wasn't sure how closely Pharma was watching me- my lab tech did make that cell phone call after I tried to print the protocols, and Tyler Stanley, who was supposed to have been "tied up" was suddenly available.

I would have to work in secret – I couldn't do anything at the university. This never came up in my trial. Pharma's lawyers didn't want to get into how I got the data because that might have suggested that my results were real, and that would have implied that there could be a problem with the drug. My lawyer thought that we should avoid bringing up my methods because they might make me look like a nut job.

Pharma tried to downplay the conflict of interest that occurred because Pharma built the lab, Pharma provided the lab tech, Pharma provided the protocols, and Pharma provided the papers. It also never came out that the lab tech was monitoring my behavior and reporting back. A big conflict of interest scandal could be just as damaging for Pharma's drug application as bad study results.

Pharma would never support my research into the cause of the liver tumors, so my inquiry became homework.

I should have said "yes" to the snake question.

"Twenty?"

"Yes, twenty."

"*Twenty. BRAWCK,*" from a large macaw behind the pet shop's counter.

The pet shop girl scrunched up her face to make it clear she was unhappy with my order.

"You have snakes?" she asked.

"No."

"But you need twenty rats?"

It would have been easier to have just answered "yes" to the snake question.

"Do you really care why I need them? If you have twenty rats, I'll take them."

She asked me to wait a minute and walked towards the rodent section. I had walked the isles before I approached her – they had plenty of rats. Cages on the top tier had Guinea pigs, teddy bear hamsters were on the middle tier (eye-level for eight-year olds), and there were two large fish tanks on the floor. The one on the left had a swarm of mice labeled "small feeders- $0.99," the one on the right was full of rats and labeled "large feeders – 1.99." The exotic reptile pet craze required a steady supply of feeder rodents.

The salesgirl and the manager talked in low voices about my request. I tried not to indicate my being able to hear them when the manager said something to her about my maybe having a fetish and not to give me any empty paper towel tubes if I asked. Asshole.

"We have them – there's no bulk discount."

"Fine."

She started grabbing rats one at a time and dropped them into a large paper bag.

"Can I get a cage large enough to hold them?"

"I don't know if we have a cage that big. How long are you going to keep them?"

I thought it over. I'd need to inject the rats every day, and then I'd need a place to put them. The rats all looked the same; I couldn't chuck them back in with the others after I shot them up. I'd lose track of who was who.

"Actually, I'll need two cages."

She gave me that look again, paused, then got two large rodent cages off a top shelf in the back of the shop.

I had her put the rats in the cages, paid, and strapped the cages into the back seat of my car. I was about two miles from the pet shop when I yelled "fuck," did a U-turn, and went back to the store.

"Do you have any food and some water bottles?"

She looked at me, annoyed, and said, "We don't have food for the rats. The rats are supposed to *be* food."

"Just give me some Hamster Chow and four water bottles."

As I got my change, the macaw behind the register said what I figured the salesgirl must have said when I left the pet shop the first time.

"Loser. Loser. BRAWCK."

I gave the bird the bird and left.

40

Twenty rats' piss smells exactly like what you would think it would smell like. I tried newspapers under the cage, but that didn't cut it. Wet cedar chips have an undesirable smell of their own, though better than the rat piss. Rats are nocturnal, and twenty rats running around all night make a lot of noise. When they spin out on the bottom of the cage, they sent cedar chips flying. My spare bedroom was not the ideal place for two months of rat experiments.

The next problem was getting the drug. I couldn't order it from Pharma, they couldn't know what I was up to. They sent a little extra with their shipments for our experiments, but most of it was pre-measured, so any pilfering would be detected by my lab tech, and she would turn me in. I thought back to the days in Underwood's lab, Steve and Martin stealing the THC stock like they were stealing liquor, the same way Ralph and I would replace vodka from his parent's liquor cabinet with tap water so the secret drinking wouldn't be detected. It was worth trying.

That would provide some of the drug, but not enough. I would need to get more.

"I'm Dr. Most from Applied Physiology," I said to the university's central stock guy. "I'm going to need an extra biohazard box for my lab."

If you have an official title – and it works even better if you have a legitimate picture ID like mine – no one questions a plausible request. The stock guy went to the back and reappeared with a small, a medium and a large sharps container. I needed one that was the same as the one hanging on the wall in the lab.

"The red one will be fine. And some 10cc syringes, thanks."

After the rats were injected with the day's medications, the needles were discarded in a sharps container, like the kind they use to dispose of needles in a hospital. Every other day a housekeeper goes around to all the labs to collect the containers and replaces them with new ones. Each syringe we used was loaded with a few extra ccs of drug to make up for measuring and administration errors. At the end of each lab day, there were at least ten syringes in the discard box, each with about 1 – 2 cc of drug still in it.

My plan was to sneak back into the lab after my tech went home but before the housekeepers got there, switch the needle box on the wall with a fresh one, collect the unused medication from the syringes, and return the now completely empty syringes to the lab in the sharps box. By repeating this every day, I would have enough drug to keep me in business.

The vodka trick worked well. There was a stock bottle of medication in the lab in case there was a problem with the pre-measured syringes, and we needed some more of the drug. The drug solution was clear, but it did have an odor, so I couldn't do a complete switcheroo. I took about half of the stock bottle off with a large syringe and replaced it with distilled water. With only half the drug removed it would still analyze out as being okay, so long as someone didn't do a precise concentration measurement. I started building my own stock of the drug.

"What smells like rat piss?"

"Rat piss."

I hadn't told Kate what I was doing, and it was her first time visiting since I opened my bedroom lab. The strength of the odor had peaked, and it was strong enough to require comment. Air fresheners just made it smell like piss and roses, so I stopped spraying.

"Come, I have something to show you." I took Kate's hand and led her to my lab.

"What are you doing, Walter?"

"You remember those rats with tumors? Pharma doesn't believe their drug is what did it, so I'm trying to prove it one way or the other."

"Why are you doing it here?"

"It's complicated. Pharma doesn't believe it, and if it is the drug, they don't want to know, so I can't do it in the lab."

"What did they say when you told them?"

"I didn't tell them about this. I don't think I can. I'd be out of a job."

"It's better *this* way? With a bedroom full of rats?"

"It's the spare bedroom, and it's only temporary. In a couple of months, they will either grow tumors or they won't, and that will be that."

"Then what will you do?"

"I'm not sure," I said.

"I'm dating an idiot."

"Anyone I know?"

We went out to dinner, and I caught her up on what had been happening with Pharma. It was good to be able to tell somebody. It was good to be able to tell her. She said she wouldn't stay at my place with the rat-piss smell, and she agreed to stay at a hotel. I decided then that if we were still together after my experiment, I would ask her to marry me. Looking back, I should have asked her before my experiment was done. Then maybe she would have stayed with me.

On the way to her hotel, I asked if we could stop back at my place so I could feed and inject the rats. She waited in the car.

"There," I said when I returned. "That didn't take too long."

"I'm so proud of you."

"Really?"

"No."

41

A watched pot never boils.

For a week, I thought I felt something when there wasn't anything to feel. The rats were tough to get a good feel of their livers; the only time I handled them was when I was getting ready to inject them, so every time I opened the cage they all went nuts- running circles, hair standing up, urine dribbling. They weren't interested in cooperating for a check of their livers. I couldn't get a good feel through the lab gloves, so I had to stay barehanded for the daily inspection. I got bit often, though never drawing blood.

The tumors showed up in the sixth week of my experiment.

The first time I felt something, I wasn't sure I had felt anything. I was prodding one of the rats' bellies, pressing with my finger as it squirmed around, and there it was. It felt like a large grain of sand under the rat's skin; it rolled over my finger and I couldn't find it again. I paused, wide-eyed, kept feeling, but I couldn't find it again. It was like when a doctor is listening to your heart and suddenly pauses and seems surprised by what he thinks he hears.

"What is it?" you'd ask.

The doctor would pause, startled at being caught in a moment of uncertainty, and say, "Oh, it's nothing."

The rat must have thought I was trying to get friendly with it, rubbing its belly deeper and harder. I was sure I had felt something, but it was gone. I was hypersensitive to it, like the princess with the pea. After a thorough exploration, I couldn't find what I thought I felt, and I put the confused rodent back in the cage.

I felt the specks for sure on a couple rats two days later. Something was definitely there. I got that nervous excitement I can only imagine people get when they check their lottery tickets and realize they have each number as it is being read off. It was rat-liver cancer, not the Powerball, but something was happening.

By the end of the last week of the second month of my home lab experiment, one rat had a convincing pea-sized nodule on its liver, and at least seven more of them had various-sized versions of the grain-of-sand-sized tumors that I had first felt.

It was settled. The drug, at least the drug in the dosage equivalents I was giving, which was close to the high dose used in the animal trials sponsored by Pharma, caused liver cancer in rats.

"It happened," I said when Kate answered the phone.

"What happened?"

"The rats…in my bedroom. They grew tumors."

"Really?"

"Yes, really. I started feeling something a few days ago, now they are coming up like Jiffy-Pop."

"What are you going to do now?"

"I don't know yet."

"Have you talked to the Pharma people?"

"I just found the first big lump. I'm not going to Pharma until the pathology comes back."

"Are they going to fire you?"

"Wouldn't you? I stole their drug, set up a lab in my guest room, and proved that their product causes cancer. Would you want me on the payroll?"

"Well, call me after you talk to them." she said.

It wasn't the best time to tell her that I loved her, but I did anyway. She let it go.

"Goodnight, Walter."

Better *Goodnight*, than *Goodbye*.

Goodbye would be later.

42

Monday morning my lab tech came into my office to tell me the manuscript from the last protocol had been posted on the web and that Tyler had called to ask if I could get it out as soon as possible.

What a joke. Research papers usually take weeks to write. They were supposed to report detailed analysis after meticulous following of experimental protocols that were carefully designed. I had over a dozen papers published, none of which I had spent more than an hour on. I read an article in one journal and didn't realize until I was almost through that I was the author. At the last faculty meeting, one of the other professors asked me about a recent article.

"I was reading last month's *Animal Research Physiology*," he said. "How important do you really think the increases in LDH are?"

He caught me off guard. "I hadn't read that one yet," I said.

"I thought you wrote it."

"Oh, I'm sorry, I thought you asked about something else..." and I bullshitted my way out of it.

I called Tyler.

"Walter, did you get a chance to look at the article we sent you today?"

"I'm looking at it now. Look, I wanted to talk to you about..."

"Good. See if you can put the rush on that one. We're hoping to see it published about the same time we announce the results of the Phase I human trials."

"The Phase I human trials," I repeated.

"Phase I is half complete. I got a friend who's an editor at the *Journal* who said he'd see what he could do about timing the release of your article to the release of our data, but he still needs the manuscript for peer review and editing before he can make any promises."

"Okay," I said, "but one thing..."

"Look, Walter, I have a meeting. Can I get back to you this afternoon? Great."

"It's the same mass."

Mike Winters set me up on the two-headed microscope again and showed me the tumor architecture. I still wasn't sure what I was looking at, but his enthusiasm made me feel as though I could make out what he said he saw.

"You sure?" I asked.

"You doubting me?"

"No. I just need to be sure."

"I take it you were hoping they wouldn't get tumors," he said.

"I don't know what I was hoping. I was hoping these rats would make me rich. Now these rats are going to put me out of a job."

"Pharma's drug?"

"Yeah"

"Bummer," he said, turning back to the microscope.

"Do me a favor," I asked him, "Can I get photos of these slides in case I need to send them anywhere?"

"Can you pay for the prints? I'm already over budget."

"Hey Walter. You got some balls experimenting behind Pharma's back like that. You're going to be an underground lab-geek cult hero for this."

"Great. Mom will be proud."

"Tyler, we have to talk. I needed to know if the rats I sent you were just a fluke or if something was up with the drug. I ran some rats of my own, 20 of them, gave them the drug, and at least eight so far have developed the same tumors."

"I see." It worried me that Tyler hadn't turned on his salesman's gab.

"So, what I'm saying is, it wasn't a bad batch of rats. I believe the drug causes liver cancer – at least in rats."

"Who knows about this?"

"Just me and a friend of mine over in pathology. What happens now?"

"Sit tight for a while, Walter. Let me talk to some of our R&D people and someone from legal and see what's the right thing to do."

I was more comforted than I should have been by Tyler's saying he wanted to do the right thing. The right thing, I guess, depends on your perspective. The right thing for whom? The right thing for Pharma? The right thing for me? The right thing for the people who were signing up for the clinical trials? How is it that the right thing can be so many different things?

I found out the truth. I passed it on. What else did I need to do? What they did with the truth was their business.

43

Tyler called the next morning.

"Walter. Our R&D people wanted me to thank you for your observations, and they wanted me to clear up any doubts you had about the project. They wanted you to know that there is nothing to worry about."

"Nothing to worry about?"

"Nothing to worry about."

"What about the cancers?"

"They are aware of the problem you found, and they have determined it was a fluke."

"A fluke?"

"A fluke."

"And nobody there is worried about using the drug in people?"

"That's just it, Walter. The studies in people are being done with the oral preparations of the drug. For the rats, it needed to be soluble for injection. They said the carrier they used is known to cause cancer in rats, but it was the cheapest and easiest way to get the drug into solution. The animals were never intended to stay alive as long as yours did, and the study end-points had nothing to do with cancer, so they didn't consider it a problem. You can't get a rat to take a pill, you know." He paused for the laughter that never came. "So you see, there is nothing to worry about as far as the tumors go."

"What carrier did they use?"

"Sorry, that's proprietary. You know the rules."

"You don't think maybe they could bend the rules this time?"

"Corporate is very sensitive to this kind of stuff. They've gotten scooped on a process before, and industrial espionage in biotech is something they look out for. They leak a secret, the next thing you know, it's published in *Nature* or a competitor beats them to market."

"I see."

"Look, if you want to go over this more with some of the science guys, there's a conference in New York in two weeks. Are you interested? I could book you a room at the Marriott Marquis. Maybe even get you *Jersey Boys* tickets."

"Let me get back to you."

"Have you seen *Jersey Boys*?"

"I *live* in New York City," Kate said. "I can't afford to do anything *in* New York City."

"I might be able to get tickets for next weekend."

"Does that mean everything is all right with Pharma?"

"They tell me it is."

"What did they say about the drug and the tumors?"

"They say it wasn't the drug, but what they mix with the drug."

I went through the whole explanation of how crystalline compounds have to be made soluble for injection – ask any cokehead. I told Kate that the people at Pharma said they were aware of the problem, but they said the problem was caused by the other chemicals, and not the drug itself. I told her they said the human trials were using the pill form and didn't include any of the cancer-causing compounds.

"*Jersey Boys*, huh," she said.

"And based on where they've sent me so far, I bet the seats are pretty good too."

"You know what just passed, Walter?"

"What?" I said. I knew.

"One year."

"Well, that works out well," I said.

We exchanged double entendres for a while, and then from out of nowhere she comes up with, "Hey. If it's what they use to make the drug soluble, why was there a dose-effect relationship?"

She had been an English major who edited manuscripts for a medium-sized New York publishing house. I knew she was smart; she was smarter than me, for sure. But still, she hadn't done any science since her freshman year of college. How the hell did she come up with that? The Pharma guys must have thought it through before coming up with what they told me. They had to repeat it amongst themselves before passing it off to Tyler to feed it to me. None of them saw that flaw, and I was ready to- if not believe it wholeheartedly - at least let it slide as an adequate explanation.

"I don't know," I said.

"You were pretty sure it was the drug that caused the tumors."

"But they said it was the carrier."

"Maybe they are just covering."

I didn't want to believe that they were lying to me, but, of course they were. The first thing Tyler had asked was if I had discussed it with anybody.

"What are you going to do?" she asked.

"I don't know, Kate. Maybe nothing. I've had enough worrying about this. I did my best to figure out what was going on. They have an explanation for what happened, and, right now, I'm willing to accept it."

"What about the people in the trials?"

"Right now, I'm just worried about what happens to me, and us."

"But the drug causes cancer."

"There are risks involved in any untested medication. Maybe the tumors only come out in rats. Maybe there is a host of side effects we don't even know about. I can't worry about that now. I did my job and I'm ready to move on."

I just wanted to get back to the weekend plans, to *Jersey Boys*, to the year being up. I wanted to be done caring about the rats and their tumors.

"Walter, do you really think that's the right thing to do?"

I lost it. "Kate, I don't know what the right thing is. I can't remember the last time I did something because it was right. You have no idea. It's all been bullshit, Kate. I haven't written a single one of the papers I've published since I got back to Midstate- Pharma did them all. All those talks I've given weren't mine – Pharma put them together. At Biotechna, all I really did was feed and water the animals while making up some data for an FDA application. When I worked for Underwood, half the stuff we said we did, we didn't do. I even cheated on that final project in Bates's class because I wanted to impress you."

It was starting to feel good. I could have kept going – confessing to things I did as a small child, but I could tell from Kate's silence that I wasn't about to receive an outflow of support.

"Walter, what are you telling me?"

"Nothing. Everything. I never thought it would come to this, but this is where I am. I don't know what to do anymore."

"Are you going to pursue the tumors with Pharma?"

"I don't think I can."

Another pause.

"Well, you're right about one thing," she said. "It has all been bullshit. I don't know what to do anymore, either. I need some time."

She hung up.

44

Most journal articles have a "methods" section. That's the part of the research paper that goes through the steps you took to perform an experiment. Ideally, someone can get a clear idea of what you did and how you did it. If people were going to trust the results, they would have to understand how they were obtained. To be valid, an experiment should be repeatable; if researchers wanted to confirm your results, they should be able to follow your methods like a recipe in a cookbook. The results they get should be similar to yours.

Most of my research papers started with something like, "We studied Sprague-Dawley rats in the research labs of our university biotechnology suite. Animals were kept in a climate controlled room with 12-hour day-night light cycles..." It always sounded clinical, well controlled, and scientific.

After Kate hung up on me, I sat in my spare bedroom thinking how I could describe my experiment to the scientific community. I imagined myself at a large research seminar presenting my results:

"Dr. Most," the bearded man with the bow-tie in the front row would begin, "your results are interesting. Could you review the study environment."

"Yes. Excellent question. The Jefferson apartment complex is essentially a series of three-story buildings housing mostly young professionals working in the upstate New York area. The experiment was performed in the spare bedroom of my apartment in Building 105. Rats were housed in a single cage from a pet shop. The cage was located on a press-board bureau, which I had purchased at WalMart and assembled while in graduate school."

"Did you receive support from the pharmaceutical company for the completion of this project?"

"Again, excellent question. Most of the pharmaceutical agents used in this project were stolen from my lab at the university. Next question..."

I could try to play along with Pharma, but there was no way they would continue to support me after what I had done. I needed a back-up plan, and again, I didn't have one. I went to the liquor store and bought a six-pack of Saranac's seasonal brew and rented *Wall Street*. After Gecko gave his "Greed is good" speech, and after the fourth of the six beers was gone, I thought I'd try writing up my experiment.

I started typing on my laptop, and finished the skeleton of the paper while I finished the last of the beers. Even though it had been years since I wrote a paper on my own, the words came quickly. The methods were simple. There was no control group. And the statistical analysis was simple enough that I could do it with my *Introduction to Biostatistics* text that I still had from college. The next morning, after working through a hangover with Motrin and orange juice, I cleaned up the parts that seemed good while I was drunk but bordered on gibberish when viewed through a sober eye. I was done with the paper in less than a week.

I still went to work every day and pushed some papers around. We were between experiments, and Pharma hadn't sent us the new protocols. They were nearly done with the animal work on the drug I was working on, and human trials had begun, so it was likely we'd just be assigned some tidying-up work for the FDA application. I doubted they were interested in sending me anything at all, except maybe a termination notice.

I spent a lot of time in the library. If I was to try to get my paper published, I would have to find a journal that might accept it. Pharma had always told me what journals I should send the papers to. An unfortunate by-product of the academic "publish or perish" mentality, combined with the enormous amount of advertising money being spent by large pharmaceutical companies, was the proliferation of scientific and medical journals - more than anyone could ever read, or would ever want to. The cycle fed itself. More advertisers could support more journals, which required more articles to justify their existence, which required more advertisers to support their number and size, which required more articles to fill... It was a perpetual increase of quantity at the expense of quality, and nobody had any idea what, if anything, could be done about it.

It was good enough for me, though. It would be impossible to get bedroom animal-drug research published in one of the major journals. I copied the *Instructions for Authors* pages from a few journals that had been on Pharma's lists in the past. I still didn't know if I would ever send it off, but at least I had some places to send it if I went ahead with it.

I still could have let it go. I still had the best lab around. If I could stay at the university, promotion would be guaranteed with all the papers I had published. Things might blow over with Kate. It had always been easy to go with the flow up until then. Why was I bucking the system? If I made up with Pharma, and the drug got approved, I could keep my fancy lab and make a few hundred grand a year helping the company promote it.

I think the last straw was the *Jersey Boys* tickets. I might have been able to ignore Kate's realization that I was being lied to. But those tickets. The offer pissed me off for two reasons. First, that they knew they could bribe me to keep my findings to myself. And second, because they knew how cheaply I could be bought.

On my way home from work, I stopped to buy more beer. Those rats had cost me Kate, and now they would cost me my career. I poured the first beer and knew it was time. I wrote the cover letter that would accompany my manuscript. I thought the best thing to do would be to send my manuscript to journals that had published my papers before.

Another mistake.

45

Two weeks after I sent out the manuscript, I received the first journal's response. By the end of the next week, I would receive rejections from all but one of the journals.

I remember senior year of high school, calling my mom from Ralph's house to see if I had received any answers from the colleges I had applied to.

"Ma, any mail?"

"What makes you think I brought it in yet?"

"Could you go get it?"

"If you're so interested in the mail, why don't you just come home and get it yourself?"

"Later. Could you check the mail?"

"You think I have nothing better to do right now than go check the mail?"

Eventually she'd get the mail.

"Anything?"

"Bill, bill, bill, junk, junk, bill. Yes, here's two letters from colleges. You want me to open them?"

"Are they thin or thick?" I'd ask.

A thick envelope would contain campus brochures, maps, parking pass instructions, student union information, a Greek life flyer, housing information, and a letter of intent to be signed and sent back with a deposit if the offer to attend the school was to be accepted. A thin envelope contained a one-paragraph letter expressing how the university would like to accept all applicants, but it couldn't, and it wouldn't be accepting you. It was always comforting, though, to be wished well in future educational endeavors.

It was the same with scientific journals. A thick envelope had author agreement letters and review comments for revisions. A thin envelope wished the authors well in getting their important work published.

The six response letters I had received in record time were wafer-thin.

There are no specific qualifications to serve on an editorial board of a scientific journal. You don't need a double PhD in molecular biology and English. Most editorial board members develop a track record of publications in a field, then they are asked to be peer reviewers. Peer reviewers are sent unedited manuscripts for opinions on whether or not an article should be published. The editorial board decides which papers are worthy of inclusion in a journal. If the editorial board likes a paper, it is sent to editorial assistants, who take care of the language and style. When the journals expand, or an editorial board member quits or dies, the remaining editorial board members offer a slot on the board to one of the peer reviewers. That's how most editorial boards are filled.

I have no way of knowing if the big drug companies actually have moles on journals' editorial boards. It would make sense for them to try. The companies would be more assured of getting articles highlighting their own drugs published and would get an early heads-up on the progress of other companies. It was usually almost a year from the time a manuscript was submitted until it was published. A year's heads-up can give a company a chance to set up a competing experiment or provide ample time to prepare a marketing response to another company's claims.

Having someone planted on an editorial board would also allow some papers to be blocked. All scientific papers have flaws. The best articles identify the flaws inherent in the research and estimate the effect these flaws may have had on the results. Authors with less integrity put spin on a paper to hide or minimize the flaws, but the flaws will be there nonetheless. Even if it were for dishonest reasons, a reviewer could find enough flaws in any particular paper to at least temporarily block its publication. It would look more like academic rigor than industrial espionage.

The delay time from submission to rejection is usually a couple of months. My experiment was conducted in my spare bedroom with pet-store rats and stolen drugs, so my chance of rejection was high. It's considered unethical to publish the same results twice. You're not supposed to submit an article to more than one journal at a time, but as I didn't think I had much time, and the chance of any journal being interested was low, I figured I could always withdraw a manuscript after it was accepted. It was considered bad form, but I no longer needed to worry about my reputation in the academic community.

I didn't get the feeling of release I was hoping for after submitting the manuscript. I was jumpy in the lab, startled with every question from my secretary or the lab tech. I used my home address as the contact address so that no one at Midstate would accidentally see something, but I still jumped on the university mail as soon as it was delivered, to prevent my lab-tech-turned-Pharma-spy from intercepting something incriminating and alerting Tyler. Fortunately, before I was barred from returning to the lab, I had gotten rid of the last of the tumor-swollen rats. I euthanized them in the usual fashion – the pentobarbital injections followed by the snapping of their necks – then I transported them in a Ziploc bag, two at a time, to the animal disposal depot at the university where they would be cremated along with the other animals that had given their lives to science.

I received notice that my article had been accepted the same day I was barred from my lab.

The day started with my usual paranoia regarding Pharma – were they watching me? Bugging my phones? Now that I have heard all the testimony against me, I can't be sure.

That day there was a sheriff posted outside the door that led to my research lab.

"I'm sorry, Dr. Most, I can't let you in. Court order."

"What do you mean?"

"I wish I could tell you more than that. I don't know myself. I just get the orders, and I do what they say." He took some folded papers from his pocket and handed them to me. "These say you are not to enter, and nothing is to be removed from this lab."

His expression indicated that while he was sympathetic, he didn't care.

"What about my stuff?"

"It says you can get personal items from your lab under supervision. You need to have your lawyer contact..." he pointed to the bottom of the paper, "this guy here, a lawyer from Pharma, and they can set up a time for you to remove any items they don't object to your removing."

"Can I go get my address book and schedule?"

"Yes. But you need to do it with the lawyers here, and without their objection."

I felt the heat come up my face. It was clear I wouldn't win the smallest victory with this guy. He was just doing his job. And he had a gun.

"I don't have a lawyer," I said, as I walked away.

He yelled as I started down the hall, "If you need a referral, my cousin's a lawyer. They say he's pretty good."

I ignored the sheriff and went to Underwood's office.

"Do you have any idea what's going on?" I asked Underwood.

"Looks like you've gotten yourself into some trouble."

"How did this happen?" I asked, thumbing towards the sheriff guarding my lab.

"The publishing community is smaller than you might think, Walter."

"Nobody at Pharma knew about the paper."

"R&D at Pharma got three separate calls from journal editors, asking them about a suspicious manuscript they had received from a Dr. Most. All three who called were editorial board members of journals you submitted to. All had been, or currently are, funded researchers for Pharma. They didn't know if you were up to anything suspicious, they were just surprised and called Pharma to find out what kind of crazy projects were being done with their products. Do you want to talk about it?"

"It's a long story." I was ready to spill the whole thing, but then I started to wonder how connected Underwood was - he knew a lot of the details. He had made his career doing research for large companies. Was he interested, or would he tell Pharma everything I told him."

"Let me guess," he said. "You found some side effect in your animals, and Pharma wasn't interested in pursuing it."

"Essentially. Some of the rats were getting tumors. It's from the drug. Pharma was starting human trials, and I thought it would be important to know."

"But you were under contract for a particular line of research. You took it upon yourself to steal from the company and perform potentially damaging experiments. Where did you do these experiments anyway?"

"The drug causes cancer."

"Walter, the truth always comes out in the end, but how it comes out matters."

"What would you have done?"

"I don't know. I can't say I've never bent the rules before, but I know not to bite the hand that's feeding me."

"What should I do now?"

Underwood paused, stroked his beard between his thumb and forefinger and said "I think you need to get a lawyer, Walter."

46

The campus legal affairs office was in the basement of the bursar's building, down a long flight of stairs. I met with one of the paralegals. The university had only two full-time lawyers, and most legal matters were farmed out to local firms.

"You put us in a tough spot, Dr. Most."

"I thought I was covered under campus legal."

The university provided free legal representation to its faculty and students. When I was an undergrad, they represented one of my fraternity brothers on a DWI. They also reviewed and approved contracts and offered legal advice and referral when the legal question was not strictly university related.

"Ordinarily, you would be," she continued. "The university would always take your side against an outside entity in a legal dispute. The problem here is that your contract with the university is contingent upon your good standing with Pharma. Your trouble with them can be interpreted as a breech of contract with the university. We certainly are not obligated to represent you if you are in breech against us. I'm sure you can understand."

The paralegal was telling me this with the same emotion I would expect if I were being told that my overnight package would take two days instead of one – like she knew I would be upset, but I shouldn't view it as a big deal in the grand scheme of things.

"I don't think you understand," I said. "They locked me out of my lab."

"Hmmm. I see how that can be a problem. I wish I could tell you something more definitive now, but I think one of the lawyers is going to have to decide what to do about this one."

Her tone shifted to that of a department store clerk who didn't want to accept a return, and was suggesting I wait for one of the managers.

She continued, "Can you give me a number where I can have one of the lawyers call you? It will probably be right after lunch."

I gave her my phone number and headed home.

The mailman was at my box when I got home, and he handed me a stack of mail. I rifled through the mail and stopped at a large waterproof envelope between a *Pottery Barn* catalog and an announcement of a clearance sale at one of the Persian rug stores that seemed to be perpetually going out of business. It was from *Physiology Discussions and Review*, the only journal I hadn't yet heard from.

I ripped it open, with the mailman still standing there. The editors had suggested some minor revisions, but they wanted to publish my paper.

"Oh, I don't believe *this*." I said, waving the envelope at the mailman.

"Good news?" he asked

"I don't know."

"OK, then. Have a nice day."

I went inside my apartment, put the mail down on the kitchen table, and pressed play on my answering machine.

"Dr. Most. This is Mark Lastman with campus legal. I've been reviewing your case, and it does look like we have a problem here. I have a complaint here from Pharma against you. It names the university as a defendant as well. It seems that we may have to consider you in breech of your contract, so we will not be able to provide you with representation in your case. You can call the office if you'd like, but right now it looks like we won't be able to be much help. You will need to get your own counsel. I hope you understand. I'm sorry. BEEP."

What was so hard to understand? I was about to be sued by the company I did research for because I discovered its product causes cancer. And because of my contract, the university wouldn't back me up.

PART 6

End of the Line

47

Kate should be here any minute now. She caught a ten-second blurb about the case on CNN and called me. It had been a while since we had spoke at all, but she called and said she'd be here before the jury came back.

"You've been having a rough time, huh," she said.

"You could say that."

"When did you decide?"

"After you left me the last time."

"Why didn't you tell me?"

"I figured you would think I was just doing it for you."

"Is that why you did it?"

"Maybe. I don't know. I just got tired."

"Tired of what?"

"The whole thing. I can handle that I haven't done, and never will do, anything important or original – most people don't, I guess. But I'd never done anything honestly either– at least not on purpose. I could have kept it up, too. The money is better in bullshit, and the work is a hell of a lot easier. It just stopped being worth it. I didn't do it just because of you, but when you left, it was all I could do."

Silence. I gave my big speech and then wondered if she'd missed it, if she hung up or got cut off.

"Kate?"

It sounded like she was crying. "Are you OK?" I asked.

"Am *I*?" she said. "You're the one doing the perp walk on CNN."

"I wasn't arrested, I'm just being sued for everything I have and more."

She laughed.

"Walter, what am I going to do with you?"

"I don't know."

"Are you alone?"

"It's just me." I thought back to college when she called after I had just finished with someone else.

"Do you have friends you can talk to? Are you seeing anyone?"

"I'm not much of a hot ticket right now. And it's impressive how quickly you lose your work friends over something silly like a restraining order."

"I'd like to come be with you."

"Are you serious?"

"Yes. I'd like to be there."

"I'd love it if you were."

The jury has the case, and Kate should be here soon.

The past year has included depositions, innumerable hours with my attorney, and now the trial. The attorney hours seem innumerable, but I know my lawyer has them well enumerated, and at $200 an hour, I've already spent more on him than on my education.

For now, the journal can't publish my paper. There have been enough leaks to the media and within the scientific community for everyone to know something is up with Pharma's drug, but the reports are sketchy. The judge determined that specific information regarding the drug was a protected industrial secret, and the press was barred from publishing any specific references to the product. In the trial transcripts, those particulars would be blacked out. For now, nobody knows.

My lawyer tells me I can go after the university for legal costs, but his meter would still be running, so it would be double or nothing. I'll decide that later.

It's been a hell of a ride, though. I was rich for a while – could have been again. I could have been well-known in the field. Now I will be well known in the field, but as a unfortunate curiosity. Maybe I can get on one of those late-night legal shows people watch with the same interest they have when they pass a highway crash.

My research career is over – that is one thing I can bank on. Who would hire me now? Sued and ruined for my first honest bit of science after a lifetime of bullshitting my way through. I spent last semester at a community college getting the credits I needed to qualify for a teaching certificate. I start subbing as a science teacher this fall. Subbing junior-high science is not the glamor job I once dreamed of, but I need some kind of second chance. Summers off are not bad either. Maybe I could learn how to sail.

"They're back."

The lead attorney for Pharma – I've learned to hate him – sticks his head out of the courtroom door to let everyone know the jury has finished deliberating.

I get up and walk towards the courtroom. The elevator *bings,* the door opens, Kate appears.

Kate to my right, Lawyer Dickhead to my left. I hope Kate sticks around after verdict because I don't have any time for her now. I'd be a good catch though – a fired, disgraced researcher who, in a couple of minutes, might join the ranks of the bankrupt.

"You're just in time," I said to her.

"Walter," Kate says, and shakes her head. "Why do I keep coming back for you?"

"If you don't know, that makes two of us." I point to the courtroom door. "We have to go in."

Kate sits in the back of the courtroom, and I join my lawyer at the defense table.

"What's that look on your face?" my lawyer asks.

I look back at Kate and then at my lawyer. My face taken over by this grin I can't shake off and my lawyer looks at me like I am crazy. At least the jury's verdict is sealed - if they saw me smiling like this while they were still deliberating, they would judge me disturbed.

"It's a long story," I tell him. "A long story."